C0-BXA-453

The Adventure of the Devilish Footnote

A New Sherlock Holmes Mystery

Note to Readers:

Your enjoyment of this new Sherlock Holmes mystery will be enhanced by re-reading the original story that inspired this one –

The Adventure of the Devil's Foot.

It has been appended and may be found in the back portion of this book.

A request to all readers:

After reading this story, please help the author and future readers by taking a moment to write a short, constructive review on the site from which you purchased the book and on Goodreads. Thank you.   CSC

ALL New Sherlock Holmes Mysteries are FREE to borrow all the time on Kindle Unlimited/Prime.

A New Sherlock Holmes Mystery

THE ADVENTURE OF THE DEVILISH FOOTNOTE

Craig Stephen Copland

The Adventure of the Devilish Footnote

A New Sherlock Holmes Mystery

Craig Stephen Copland

Copyright © 2020 by Craig Stephen Copland

All rights reserved. No part of this book may be reproduced or transmitted in any form or by any means, electronic or mechanical, including photocopying, recording, or by an information storage and retrieval system – except by a reviewer who may quote brief passages in a review to be printed in a magazine, newspaper, or on the web – without permission in writing from Craig Stephen Copland.

The characters of Sherlock Holmes and Dr. Watson are no longer under copyright, nor is the original story, *The Adventure of the Devil's Foot.*

Published by:

Conservative Growth Inc.
3104 30th Avenue, Suite 427
Vernon, British Columbia, Canada
V1T 9M9

Cover design by Rita Toews
ISBN: 9798555415813

Dedication

To the present-day descendants of the Bloomsbury Group: the artists, writers, critics, theorists, intellectuals and economists who do their best to help the rest of us make sense of our world.

Contents

Acknowledgments

All of us, the company of Sherlockians around the globe who continue to write new stories about our hero, owe our everlasting gratitude to Sir Arthur Conan Doyle for his creation of Sherlock Holmes and Dr. Watson and for the sixty original stories of The Canon. This new story was inspired by *The Adventure of the Devil's Foot*.

My friends and colleague in my two online writers' groups—the Buenos Aires English Writers and the Vernon Writers Critique Group—endured numerous rough drafts of chapters of this story. Their suggestions and corrections were invaluable. So also were the edits and insights of my writing buddy, Geoff White, who meets with me every Friday for lunch at our local Denny's, where we dissect what we have written that week.

Two of my very supportive readers, Cheryl Adamkiewiczm of Rockwood, Tennessee and Teresa Snipes of Winter Garden, Florida voluntarily provided extensive copy editing and proofreading. Thank you.

My dearest friend, partner of many years and now wife, Mary Engelking, and my big brother, Dr. James Copland continue to review and critique everything I create before I dare think of publishing it.

Three of my readers—Frank Felton of Florida, Sheree Sheridan of Maryland, and Mary Williams of Michigan—courageously volunteered to allow me to use their names and characters in this story. Thank you.

.

Chapter One

Turned to Port

She was one of those woman poets with blue-tinted silver hair and three names, and she had used her inherited wealth to support no end of struggling writers and literary endeavors. The news of her unexpected death spread like a contagion through those circles of London who considered themselves to belong to the higher echelons of artistic knowledge and refinement.

However, it could not be said that the passing of Lady Gwendolyn Ottoline Carrington was met with an outpouring of grief and heartache.

The critic for *The Telegram,* a Mr. Harley de J. Descatoire, upon hearing the news whilst sipping absinthe in the bar of the Duke of Hastings Hotel in Knightsbridge, exclaimed, "Will not we all miss her pennies so dearly, her personality only somewhat, and her poetry not at all?"

When it became known that she had been murdered, the same self-appointed arbiter of literary taste pronounced, "I rather suspect that a clever barrister could deliver a convincing argument for a case of justifiable homicide. And, well, there could be no more than a hundred probable suspects, every one of whom could claim he acted in self-defense. Honestly, you do know, don't you, that her poetry was enough to drive any sensitive aesthete to slit his wrists."

* * *

"How did she die?" I asked Sherlock Holmes as an early morning cab hurried us from Baker Street to the house in Bermondsey in which Her Ladyship had lived.

"The note from Lestrade only said that she was poisoned. He demanded that we come immediately and will be waiting for us at the house. You're a writer, Watson. Do you know anything about this woman?"

"I hardly move in the same circles. She was the Doyen of the Bermondsey Set and owned and published the *Cornwall Monthly Review*. It is one of the very few journals to pay its writers and does so handsomely. The stories and poems that appear in it are excellent, with the exception of her own poems, one of which she inserts in every issue. Beyond that, I cannot tell you much."

The streets of London were still empty at five o'clock in the morning of 10 June in the first year of the new century. It had rained heavily during the night, giving the macadam and concrete that distinct fresh, damp smell that would linger only until the horses and carriages and motor cars of London were let loose.

By way of the Westminster Bridge, we raced across the Thames, swollen and muddied from the rain, and wove our way through Southwark. As we bumped and hurried, I took a long look at Mr. Sherlock Holmes. He was wide awake, although his eyes were closed. He had tented his fingers under his chin and was moving his lips and nodding his head, oblivious to the beginning of a new day.

Our cab reached the Bermondsey Wall Road. Holmes's eyes were now open, and he was looking out the cab window. The section of London we had entered was a notch above Southwark but still far from prosperous. The bank of the Thames was lined with wharves, and most of the buildings adjacent to them were warehouses, granaries, industrial yards and public houses.

"Odd," I commented, "that this lady would live here rather than in Mayfair or Belgravia. She certainly had enough money to own a home, or two for that matter, in the rich neighborhoods."

"I believe you will find," said Holmes, "that there is a certain postured pride amongst members of the ruling cultural nobility that considers it fashionable to live in a poorer neighborhood and pretend to be in sympathy with the working class. They consider themselves to be ardent supporters of all good labor and socialist causes and, being the recipients of sufficient inherited wealth or remittances, can afford to do so."

"Whilst not working themselves," I added.

"Precisely."

We arrived at a short stretch of somewhere-between-red-and-orange terraced houses that had a clear view of the Thames. The breeze, the vista of the open water beyond the wharves and, in the distance, the piers and quays of Wapping, were rather pleasant on an early summer day. We may have been in a less-prosperous part of London, but this street was on the not-all-that-badly-off edge of it.

The view from one of the houses was now blocked by the two police wagons parked in front of it. Uniformed constables stood on either side of the door like caryatid columns, and a handful of curious neighbors were clustered on the pavement. Holmes has a longstanding aversion to publicity and he circumvented the lot of them. I heard the name of Sherlock Holmes being muttered as we strode past and entered the house.

Chief Inspector Lestrade greeted us in the entryway.

"This one is right up your alley, Holmes," he said. "One woman dead and another almost. Six people could have done her in, not to mention her staff. Come in and take a look. And don't ask me if I have made sure nothing was disturbed. All we did was draw the drapes."

"I would never have suspected otherwise," said Holmes. "Please enlighten me with such details as you have."

The front room of the house was graced by a large bay window that would have provided a grand view of the River Thames had the curtains not been completely drawn. The reason for their being so was obvious. In an armchair, situated directly in front of the window, sat the body of Lady Gwendolyn Ottoline Carrington. Had the curtains been open, the neighbors would have had an unobstructed look at her.

Except for the now grey hue of her skin and the slight bluish tinge appearing on her lips, she looked to be perfectly at peace. She was a handsome woman of fifty-some years. Every strand of her silver-blue hair was firmly in place. Her clothing affected a Bohemian flair vaguely similar to what one imagined peasants might wear in the Carpathians if they could afford fine wool and perfect tailoring.

On the floor at her feet lay a tan-colored cocker spaniel. It was resting its head on her shoes and whimpering.

"What we've learned so far is this," said Lestrade. "The lady liked to host gatherings in the evening. *Soirées* they call them. You know, Holmes, the type of party where the hoity-toity literati get together and read poems and stories to each other and do all that titter-titter, chat-chat, clap-clap, and then gobble up the free food the host has laid out."

"I cannot say I have ever been invited to such an event," said Holmes. "Although, I believe Dr. Watson is familiar with them."

I grunted a reply and added, "The editors at the *Strand* have been known to throw one or two from time to time. Please continue, Inspector."

"Right. Well, there was a fair crowd of them, and they all helped themselves to the food and liquor. You can see the bottles on the sideboard. Hardly a heeltap left. And around half-past nine, most of them depart. Six remain—her inner circle of writers. Well, seven if you count the child. Around ten, the woman who manages her household brings out a bottle of Port. They chat until ten-thirty. Then they all leave. The lady decides she wants a glass of Port before going off to bed, and so has her secretary pour one for her and one for herself. The lady, it seems, is more than a little fond of her chosen libation and polishes the glass off in a few minutes. The secretary who, I was told, is also the editor of the journal, is more constrained, and she sips slowly. Then it looks like the lady falls asleep in her chair, but the secretary says she suddenly began to feel nauseated and rushes off to the lavatory to drink some water, and having swallowed several cups, she vomits violently and passes out. When she comes to—by now it's past midnight—she's feeling like she was run over by a train and stumbles back out to the parlor and finds Her Ladyship deader than last month's lettuce. She staggers out to the street and screams for a police officer. He arrives, and he sends for me. I get here, and I send for you. And that's the long and short of it, Holmes. Feel free to look around. I know you're dying to do so, if you'll excuse the expression."

Holmes went to work straight away and picked up the two stemmed crystal glasses that were sitting on the side table. He held the near-empty one up to his nose and then the second, which was still half-full.

"Cyanide," he said. "Quite a strong mixture but hard to detect over the aroma of the Port. Several swallows would be more than enough to kill someone, and a sip enough to make one very ill."

He held up the bottle of fine Port to the light and then sniffed the mouth of the bottle.

"This is almost empty. Surely she did not drink all of it."

"That's where it gets complicated, Holmes," said Lestrade. "The house manager says that the bottle was opened toward the end of the evening, and several of the guests drank some of it. But not one of them is dead on the floor or out on the street, and no reports of any of them waking up dead this morning, at least not so far. Looks like someone must have slid the poison into the bottle just before leaving."

"Was it her habit to take a glass of Port before retiring for the night?" asked Holmes.

"I'm told she did it every night and insisted that her secretary join her. It looks like whoever did her in did not care if he—or she, there were women here—killed another woman at the same time."

"With your permission, Inspector, I will examine the room and the rest of the house."

"It's all yours."

"And the secretary? Is she still in the house?"

"The staff got her up to a bedroom. She's there, and you can talk to her if you want. Her name's Mildred Smith, and we already questioned her. She's in pretty poor shape, but go ahead if you think it would help."

Chapter Two

It's Been a Long Time

I had expected that Holmes would take out his glass and start with his customary close inspection of the room. He surprised me by leaving and proceeding directly to the staircase.

"Holmes," I said as I scampered up after him. "Now, you go easy on this woman. She likely retched repeatedly to expel the cyanide. She does not need you upsetting her before she has recovered."

"I will be as calm and tactful as I always am."

"That is what I am afraid of. Please try to be considerate. She was very nearly a collateral victim of whoever killed her employer."

He stopped and looked down at me.

"My dear Watson, we do not yet know that she was merely an accidental bystander to the murder. It is possible that the killer intended to poison them both. For that matter, we do not know that she was not the primary target and that the lady was the unfortunate unintended victim. It is a capital mistake—,"

"Yes, Holmes, you do not have to remind me. But let me remind you. I am a doctor, and this woman is in severe medical distress. You will not make her condition worse."

He looked directly at me. "Your point is taken, my friend. I will do my best not to alarm her."

The bedroom to which we were directed looked out over the Thames. It was unusually furnished with a sturdy dark oak desk and bookshelves, a large bed with an oak headboard and footboard, and a long leather sofa. The paintings on the wall were set in Africa and showed scenes of Mount Kilimanjaro, the Serengeti, and of hunters in pith helmets standing triumphantly over the carcasses of zebras, antelope, and a leopard. The head of an antelope with stunning twisted horns was mounted on the wall across from the bed.

In the bed, a woman of about forty years was sitting up, supported by several pillows. Her dark hair, sprinkled with a few strands of grey, was down and spread out over her shoulders. Her finely sculpted face was ghastly pale, accentuated by the black silk blouse and a necklace of gleaming white pearls. Her left arm lay limp on the far side of her body, the glint from a large amethyst ring twinkling from the bedclothes. Sitting beside her on a chair and holding her other hand was an older woman in a nurse's uniform. As we entered, the nurse let go of the hand and stood and blocked our access to the bed.

She was tall, and her nurse's cap and eyeglasses gave her a rather commanding presence.

"Good morning," said Holmes. "I am sorry to have to trouble you. My name is Sherlock Holmes. I am a consulting detective—"

"Miss Smith is in no condition to receive visitors," the nurse informed us. "Kindly leave and come back—"

"It is quite all right, Mrs. Sheridan," said the woman in the bed. "I may as well talk to Sherlock Holmes and get it over with. The inspector told me you were coming, Mr. Holmes. I know who you are. I've read all those stories Dr. Watson writes about you."

As the nurse stepped aside, her patient looked at me, and a faint smile crept across her wan face.

"Hello, John. It's been a long time."

"It has Millie," I said. "It's good to see you again, although I wish it were not under these circumstances."

"You and me both."

It is not often that anything I do leaves Holmes with his mouth open in surprise.

"You two have met each other before?" he said.

I bit my tongue and refrained from remarking on the brilliance of his deduction.

"Miss Smith once worked at Beeton's," I said, "and we got to know each other when I submitted my first story to them years ago. We both moved on, and now our paths cross again. I was not surprised to hear of her success helping Lady Carrington with the *Cornwall Review*."

"Nor I," she said, her voice weak but clear, "to see you become one of England's most popular writers. How have you been?"

Holmes forced a cough to interrupt the conversation, and I knew he was determined to get on with his interview.

"We have," I said, "much to talk about. Let's let Mr. Holmes get through his questions first, shall we?"

"Oh, very well, if we must, we must. What does Sherlock Holmes want to know?"

"Thank you, madam," said Holmes. "Allow me to begin with the events of last evening."

He then posed several questions to her, and she recounted, wearily, what had happened. Her version was the same as we had heard from Lestrade. In a feeble attempt to lighten her mood, Holmes made an ill-advised quip about the unforgivable crime of ruining a bottle of fine Port.

Miss Smith was not amused.

"Mr. Holmes," she said, "I am not in the mood for droll humor. The woman for whom I worked for nearly twenty years was murdered and may still be sitting dead in a chair a floor below me. I came very close to being murdered by the same killer. Forgive me if I am not laughing."

"My apologies, madam. I appreciate what you have endured. I will try to conclude my questions as quickly as possible and let you rest."

Then Holmes became more specific.

"According to the police, several of the guests also drank from the same bottle of Port before departing."

"They did, yes," Miss Smith answered.

"Did all of the guests leave at the same time, or did some of them depart earlier?"

"Oh, now, I really cannot say for certain. Can you help with that, Mrs. Sheridan?" she said, looking at the nurse.

"Were you," said Holmes, now also looking at the nurse, "whoever you are, present throughout the evening?"

She nodded. "I was. My name, Mr. Holmes, is Mrs. Sheree Sheridan, and I have been Lady Carrington's nurse and personal assistant for the past seven years. Miss Smith looked after her publications, and I managed the household."

"Then, if you were present last evening, perhaps you can answer my question."

"I can, yes. Lady Williams departed just after nine-thirty, and Reverend Chrisparkle at fifteen minutes to ten. The remainder of the guests stayed until twenty-five minutes past ten, and they all departed the house at that time."

"And do you have the list of the guests who attended?"

"I do, sir. I have already prepared it for the inspector. I can write out one for you too."

"Thank you, Mrs. Sheridan. That would be very useful."

He now turned back to Mildred Smith.

"I assume that all of the guests were friends, at least to some extent, of Lady Carrington. Is that correct?"

"No, Mr. Holmes. It is not correct. Lady Gwendolyn Ottoline Carrington was a capable business-woman, but she did not have friends unless you count her dog. She had sycophants, minions, toadies, bootlickers, dependents, and no end of obsequious flatterers. She collected and cultivated them and made them dependent for their financial sustenance on the generous payments and royalties she doled out. Would you agree, Mrs. Sheridan?"

"For the most part, yes."

"Is that so?" said Holmes. "And what happened if one of them ceased to flatter her?"

"They were cut off," said Miss Smith, "and became impoverished and had to go elsewhere to sell their stories and poems. They quickly learned that no one else in London paid anywhere near as well as our *Cornwall Monthly Review.*"

"Indeed? Well, thank you for being so frank and concise. Now, I must ask a pointed question, and I assure you that whatever you say will be kept in strictest confidence. In your judgment, did any of the guests hold such an animus toward Lady Carrington that they would wish to see her dead?"

"Mr. Holmes," said Miss Smith, "they all *wished* that she were dead and gone. But they are writers and poets and critics and editors. All they ever do is imagine murdering someone and writing about it. They are not people capable of doing dastardly deeds themselves. Far from it. Although it now seems that one of them was, and I would be very grateful if you can determine who it was as I am not feeling very kindly toward him … or her."

"I will do my best, I assure you."

He paused for a moment and looked around the room.

"One final question, if I may. Whose bedroom is this?"

Holmes had reached the same conclusion I had upon entering. We were in a room frequented by a man, not a woman. Her Ladyship's bedroom was located at the other end of the hall and was, I assumed, furnished and decorated in the stylish manner to be expected of a woman who believed herself to have an artistic temperament.

Miss Smith did not immediately answer, and I had the impression she was choosing her words carefully before doing so.

"Her Ladyship," she said, "was a reliable and generous employer to me for many years. I do not wish to injure her reputation now that she is no longer with us."

"Your loyalty," said Holmes, "and consideration are most commendable, and I do not claim any expertise in the literary world. However, I have observed enough to assure you that attaching a whiff of scandal to her name would enhance the sales of your journal and render her poetry mandatory reading in our universities for years to come. As she is no longer with us, you cannot possibly do her any injury by informing me as to who was her frequent house guest."

She looked over at the nurse, and the two of them shrugged and nodded.

"For the past year or two," said Mrs. Sheridan, "she has been engaged in a romantic friendship with a gentleman. He stays here when he is in London."

"His name, please."

"Dr. Leon Sterndale."

Chapter Three

The Great Lion Hunter

I stopped taking notes. Holmes stopped asking questions. We looked at each other. He recovered first.

"And is this man," he asked, "Sterndale, you say, here in London?"

"He arrives tomorrow from Cape Town," said Mrs. Sheridan. "His last telegram said that he will come here straight away after disembarking. He will not have heard about what has happened."

"That will be a dreadful shock to him," I said. "When will he get here?"

"His ship, the *Dunottar Castle,* pulls into the East India Docks at seven. He should be here by ten."

Holmes asked, "Was there a reason for his return at this time? Were they contemplating marriage, perhaps?"

"Marriage, no," said Mrs. Sheridan. "It was about his story, wasn't it, Millie?"

"His story?" said Holmes. "Was this man a writer?"

"That depends on whom you ask," said Miss Smith. "If you asked Her Ladyship, he was the most exciting thing to come along since Dick Turpin. If you asked anyone with any literary taste, he was just another Penny Dreadful scribbler."

I was fascinated. I knew that Holmes was impatient to get more information about the deceased's friends, lovers and sycophants, but I was intrigued to learn that Dr. Leon Sterndale, the famous African big-game hunter with whom we had a frightening encounter three years ago, was also an author.

"Did you read his story?" I asked Mildred Smith. "What did he write about?"

"It was an utterly absurd tale about some rich husband and domineering wife who set off on a hunting safari to Africa, accompanied by some brute of a guide. The husband shoots a lion but only wounds it, and then, quite sensibly, turns tail and runs away when the lion charges. The guide has to shoot the lion. The wife considers the husband a coward and has an affair with the guide. The next day a mad buffalo charges at them, but the husband has found his courage and shoots it. Then the wife, knowing that she has lost control of her husband, shoots him. It is the most ridiculous drivel I have ever read. Our readers will hate it. But Her Ladyship insisted, and Dr. Sterndale agreed to come back from Africa to be here when it was published. She was going to throw a party in his honor."

She had become animated whilst giving this account and seemed to collapse in weariness when she had finished. The nurse intervened.

"Mr. Holmes, Dr. Watson, I must insist that you leave Miss Smith now and let her get some rest. I suggest that you return tomorrow if you wish to pursue your questioning."

As she spoke, she moved to stand between Holmes and me and the bed, leaving no doubt what we were to do next. We bade the women a gracious good day and started to leave the room when one of them called out.

"John!"

I turned back. "Yes, Millie."

"John, can I ask a small favor?"

"By all means. Anything."

"Would you mind taking Pilot with you when you leave?"

"Who?"

"Her spaniel. He's a friendly little fellow, and he has no one else to look after him. Please, John. Would you mind terribly?"

"Happy to help," I lied.

Partway down the stairs, Holmes took hold of my forearm, and we stopped.

"My dear Doctor, forgive my prying into your past, but between you and Miss Smith, I detected something of a warmth from a time long ago. Might that be true?"

I shrugged. "Well, yes, you could call it that. We got to know each other back when I submitted my first story to Beeton's. She edited it—rather brilliantly, I must admit—and turned it from a semi-literate jumble of words into quite a good account. I suppose I can brag a little about it since, after all, it was all about you."

"Ah, yes, *A Study in Scarlet*. I remember it well. She improved it, you say. And it seems that whilst this was happening, there might have been some amorous feelings pass between the two of you."

"Briefly, yes. But she was determined to excel as an editor, and Lady Carrington poached her away to help her launch her *Cornwall Review*. She has been the editor of the journal ever since."

"But why did you not pursue your interest in her?"

"We differed sharply over an issue that is long forgotten. Then she moved to Cornwall, and I lost contact with her. Shortly thereafter, I met Mary Morstan."

Holmes looked puzzled.

"But why would she go there? Can any good literary thing come out of Cornwall?"

I did not immediately reply, as I quickly made a list in my mind of several novelists and poets who hailed from Cornwall. They had all, understandably, moved to London, unlike Mildred Smith, who had gone in the other direction. The obvious answer to Holmes's question was not hard to provide.

"Because that is where Lady Carrington lived at the time. She had inherited a large family estate that abutted the Duchy of Cornwall properties and announced that she would devote hundreds of pounds to the establishing of a top-drawer monthly review. A few years on, she saw the light, and the two of them moved back to London."

"Ah, yes, quite understandable."

We entered the parlor, and I saw immediately that the curtains had been opened, allowing the morning sun to stream into the room. The body of Her Ladyship had been removed, and the cocker spaniel was now sitting in the chair in which she had died. He was looking out the window, motionless.

I expected that Holmes would want to speak to Lestrade and compare thoughts and notes with him. The inspector was standing in the front room and chatting with two uniformed constables and another inspector who I did not remember having seen before.

"Ah, there you are, Holmes," said Lestrade. "I would like you to meet Inspector Frank Farber. He's with the Military Mounted Police and just back from the Cape. Jones has gone to join them for six months. A sort of cross-pollination program. This is his first case with Scotland Yard."

The fellow was about my height and aspect and near to both Holmes and me in age. His trim physique, close-cropped hair, and pencil mustache had BEF written all over him.

"And an honor," said this inspector, "to work not only with Scotland Yard but also with the famous Mr. Sherlock Holmes and Dr. Watson."

He and I shook hands with the immediate familiarity of two men who had both served Her Majesty under fire.

"Afghanistan," he said, "if I remember correctly. The Northumberland Fusiliers? Yes?"

"It was," I said. "A long time ago."

I liked this fellow and bade him welcome, and then, just in the way of friendly chat, asked him when he had come back to England.

"Only three days ago. Not even time to get used to the weather. The Cape is paradise by comparison."

"And a pleasant voyage?" I said, remembering the only time I had come back to England by way of rounding the Cape.

"Oh, yes. Quite pleasant. I recall reading that you sailed on the *Orentes*. I had a much easier time of it. I was on the Union-Castle Line. The voyage was—"

"Which ship?" said Holmes, rudely interrupting the man.

The military policeman looked somewhat offended for a moment, but then, as if he remembered that Sherlock Holmes was known for being abrupt, calmly replied.

"A lovely new vessel, the *Dunottar Castle*."

Chapter Four

The Six Suspects

We carried on chatting to the two inspectors until Mrs. Sheridan entered and gave Holmes the list of attendees at the soirée. He glanced at it briefly and handed it on to me.

"It appears we have six suspects," I said. "Well, only four if we knock off the two who left early."

I felt three pairs of eyes looking at me.

"My dear Watson," said Holmes, "if we are dealing with a murderer who would not care if he, or she, killed one extra person, then we have to assume that he, or she, would not have cared if two or three or four more just happened to die as well." He glanced at the police inspectors. "Would you agree, gentlemen?"

They nodded.

"One of these writers," said Lestrade, "is hiding an evil killer under the affected guise of a Bohemian scribbler."

"If you will allow me to add," said Inspector Farber, "it remains a possibility not only that the murderer did not care if several people died, it may have been his intention."

"Or *her* intention," added Holmes. "Which compels us not to forget to ask who amongst the staff were present?"

"The cook had gone after serving supper," said Lestrade. "You met the nurse who serves as her personal manager upstairs. There was a young maid who helped serve and clean up, and then she walked home. She showed up here this morning just before you two arrived, collapsed into hysterics, and had to be helped home by one of my constables. Frankly, given her abundance of mental vacuity, I doubt the simple thing could even spell *cyanide,* let alone know how to procure it. So, I think it safe to leave her off the list."

We chatted some more, and then we departed. Holmes stopped on the front steps.

"You forgot something," he said.

"Right," I sighed, and I returned to the parlor for the cocker spaniel. I made a quick dash up the stairs to the bedroom and stuck my head into the room.

"Millie, I will be in touch."

"Thank you, John," she said, "and please don't forget—"

"I'm taking him with me."

I hastened back to the parlor and the chair by the window.

"C'mon there, Pilot, you literary old fellow," I said, knowing that I was carrying on a conversation with a canine. "You're coming with me."

Pilot did nothing more than raise his head and stare at me with sad, dark eyes. I leaned over and put my arms under him and lifted, hoping that he would not object and growl. He made no move other than a small wiggle to get comfortable in my arms, and we walked out of the house. The two police inspectors mumbled a few words of thanks and approval as I carried him, and I was tempted to ask if

Scotland Yard wished to question the witness before I removed him from the scene, but thought better it.

Holmes was now waiting in a cab, and I lifted Pilot in and laid him on the floor. He didn't move.

Once we were on our way, I turned to Holmes and to the case at hand.

"That Dr. Sterndale chap is here now in London."

"Indeed, he is."

"But he told them that he was arriving tomorrow. Why would he deceive them?"

"An excellent question, Watson."

"Do you think he could have murdered the lady? He was an expert on exotic poisons. And he did not hesitate to do away with … what was his name? … Mortimer Tregennis."

"He was indeed, and not likely."

"Not likely what?"

"That he killed the woman. As far as we know, he was not present last night when the cyanide was put into the bottle of Port. He would not hesitate to kill again, I am sure. However, his attitude to women to whom he had a romantic attachment was one of caring and protection. I would be more worried about what he might do to whomever he believes did murder his latest paramour."

"Oh, yes," I said, "well, whoever did it will not be long for this earth if Sterndale finds out."

"Best we find out before he does."

"What are you going to do?"

"I will spend the rest of the day today learning everything I can about the people who attended the event last night. Then tomorrow, I shall start to pay calls on them. If you can be free to accompany me, I would find your help useful."

"Ready, aye, ready," I said and then said nothing until we were closer to Baker Street, when I casually added, "Speaking of useful help, a thought occurred to me."

"You thought that we should recruit those two women to help."

"Why, yes. How did you know that?"

"To be more specific, what you really want is an opportunity to renew your friendship with Miss Mildred Smith, and having me ask her to help us would make that possible and not look as if you were paying undue attention to her. Asking the older woman, Mrs. Sheridan, as well also deflects your interest in … what did you call her? Millie?"

"Holmes. I object. Whatever interest and intentions I might have are entirely honorable."

"Of course, they are, my friend. You are incapable of doing anything else. And I agree. She is quite the brilliant woman, and you have been on your own for far too long since losing your beloved Mary."

Holmes got out of the cab at Baker Street, and I continued on to my medical practice. I carried Pilot in and laid him on the floor at the feet of my receptionist. Somewhat apologetically, I asked if she would mind making a quick run to the High Street and buying a sack of whatever passed for dog food these days. She looked daggers at me and agreed.

Mrs. Hudson was likewise not thrilled when I arrived back at 221B and deposited an aging dog on the rug in front of the hearth.

At seven o'clock the following morning, I rose and prepared myself for the day. My pockets bulged with extra notebooks and pencils, and I was ready to charge into intellectual sparring matches with the members of the Bermondsey Set.

When I descended from my bedroom, Holmes was already sitting at the breakfast table, sipping on a coffee. There was a stack of files and notes beside him that, I assumed, contained data on the six people who had been in Lady Carrington's home the night before last. He gestured to the other chair and poured me a cup.

"These writerly people," he said, picking up the files, "are rather odd ducks. All lean toward socialism and pacifism. Not the most sensible folk but hardly given to killing off their enemies. They labor under the self-centered delusion that the pen is mightier than the sword and prefer to skewer their opponents with nasty insults than engage in honest fisticuffs. However, none seem at all inclined to murder two women. Do you know anything about them?"

"I might if you tell me who they are."

He opened the first file. "First up is *Mademoiselle* Marie Louise de la Suavée. That, however, is not her true name. She is from Bury and was known as Mary Louise Salmon until she moved to London. She is a young poetess who writes a poem a day and has one or two of them published in the *Cornwall Review* every two months. It may be her entire source of income, and she lives lavishly as a permanent guest at the Langham."

"I have," I said, "read her poems, the ones that were published. She also uses the pen name of *Ouinon* and is rather talented."

"If you say so. She is followed by the Reverend Edward Chrisparkle, a puritanical scribbler of religious tracts."

"What is he doing in that crowd?" I asked.

"He contributes a page every month called *Our Monthly Bread* in which he writes an uplifting message based on Holy Writ and explained in such a way as to make the reader feel somewhat more compelled to act charitably toward the rest of the human race. His page may be all that keeps the journal from being condemned outright by the Lord Chamberlain or whoever it is in Whitehall who has such power over printed publications. His antithesis is Clive Merryweather Clapper, who writes intelligent and informed reviews of books and plays in the outrageous style of Walter Pater. I would ignore him entirely except that I discovered he is the step-brother of Lady Carrington."

"I've heard some rumors about him. They say he is of a somewhat alternative persuasion when it comes to his romantic interests."

"You heard correctly. However, he does have a fifteen-year-old daughter who was with him that evening."

"Ah, that was the child Lestrade referred to. So, she would be Lady Carrington's niece, right? But if he is the brother, why is he not Lord Carrington?"

"I did not say he was the legitimate step-brother. Now we come to Mr. Saxon Sydenham, who seems to be the only man in the group who has significant independent wealth and is not on the payroll of Her Ladyship's journal. He does not appear to write anything except for cheques and invoices. The other woman who lays claim to a title is Lady Mary Williams, a childhood friend of Lady Gwendolyn from Cornwall. They grew up together and have been creative compatriots since their teen years."

"Ah yes," I said, "she writes biographies of scandalous historical women and heart-breaking romance stories of loves lost in exotic places. The women of England are terribly fond of them."

"So I am told. I take it you have not read them. Or perhaps one or two?"

"One or two, yes, some time ago. Currently, she is writing about Lucrezia Borgia. A rather titillating account, I have heard. That leaves one more, does it not?"

"Yes, and I have saved him until the end. Mr. Thoby MacCarthy is, by all accounts, a thoroughly unliked fellow. He writes brilliant short stories. What do you call them? *Roman à clef?* Thinly disguised satirical fiction in which the vice and folly of everyone who might appear in the society pages are held up to ridicule. Nobody likes him at all. He engages in feuds with all and sundry, including her late-ladyship. He is, therefore, my primary suspect. Now we have to move quickly and have friendly chats with them all."

"Are you not going to try and find Dr. Sterndale?"

"Why bother? I fully expect that he will find me. Another cup of coffee?"

He poured out a second cup, and we spent a few more minutes chatting about the list of attendees. I had just finished my coffee when the bell at the door on Baker Street rang. It was followed by a vigorous knocking, which ascended into a distinct pounding.

Holmes put down his cup and, with a smug smile, leaned toward the door.

"Mrs. Hudson!" he called out. "Would you be so kind as to get the door? And please welcome Dr. Sterndale. Let him know that we are expecting him."

Heavy footsteps quickly marched up the stairs. A thick, powerful-looking man stomped into the room and banged his gnarled ebony walking stick on the floor.

"How the devil did you know it was me?" he demanded. "I made sure that no one knew I was coming to see you."

"That is what you should expect when you pay me an anonymous visit, Dr. Sterndale. Please, sir, sit down. Coffee? Perhaps some breakfast?"

"No, blast you, Holmes. What I want is information. What do you know about who murdered Gwendolyn?"

"Only what you read in the paper this morning. That was what brought you to my door, was it not?"

"You know it was. Is it true that Scotland Yard has engaged your services?"

"That is what the Press reported, was it not? As we all know, they would never mislead their readers."

"Do you know who killed her?"

"No."

"But you are going to find out, right?"

"Yes."

"Good, then I am going to help you."

"No."

"Why not?"

"Because, my dear Doctor, I do not want you to become a law to yourself again and go and kill my prime suspect before I have a chance to have him, or her, convicted."

"Fine, then I will go it alone."

He put down his unfinished cup of coffee and rose to his feet.

"A question," said Holmes, "before you go, if you do not mind."

"What?"

"Were you in love with Lady Carrington as passionately as you were with Brenda Tregennis?"

The great African hunter's face softened. He sat back down in his chair and poured himself another cup of coffee.

"No…I was not. That depth of love comes only once in a lifetime. Gwendolyn and I were cut from the same cloth. It was a romantic friendship of convenience. We got along. We were going to go and live together in the Cape after she disposed of her journal."

I saw Holmes's eyebrow twitch, but he continued his line of questioning.

"But you could not marry her, as you are already married."

"The colonies, Mr. Holmes, are like New York. No one cares who is married to whom, or not. As long as you have enough money and a bombastic presence, you can live however you wish."

"Ah, yes. I would not know that. But if you cared at all for this woman, pray tell why did you deceive her and tell her you were arriving in London today when you arrived here three days ago?"

Dr. Sterndale leapt to his feet. "You are the devil himself! How did you know that?"

His fierce face turned to a dusky red, his eyes glared, and the knotted, passionate veins started out in his forehead,

"Really, my dear man, sit down," said Holmes. "One only has to glance at the ships' arrival and departures notices to see that only one liner has arrived this week from the Cape. But that is beside the point.

Why would you lie to the woman you had invited to come and live with you?"

Sterndale sat down and took a slow sip of coffee that had now cooled.

"I had private business here that I did not wish to disclose to her."

"Regarding your wife?"

"Confound you, yes, I asked her again to consent to a divorce, and she refused. Bigamy, they say, is having one wife too many. And so, it seems, is monogamy."

"Although," said Holmes, "it is too late to be of any use to you, I recommend the advantages of remaining a bachelor. But allow me to add that given your interest in this case, I will need to keep in contact with you. Where are you staying, as I assume you will not be moving into your bedroom in Bermondsey?"

That brought a startled look from Dr. Sterndale, but he relaxed and then slowly stood up.

"I own a house in Fitzrovia."

"Where your wife lives."

"I do not care who lives there. I own it. I will be staying there."

He rose and, in considerable ill-humor, strode slowly down the stairs and out to Baker Street.

"Well, Watson," said Holmes, "I fear that London is somewhat more dangerous a place to live than it was a week ago with that man on the loose."

"Are you going to warn the others?"

"I think not. While a desire for vengeance does move a man like him to action, it tends to cloud his reason. He may prowl the streets of London like a roaring lion, seeking whom he may devour, but I expect he will end up hungry. I shall turn my attention to gathering insights on our list of suspects."

"Starting with that nasty Thoby MacCarthy chap?"

"Heavens no. I have followed your very useful suggestion of recruiting the assistance of two very capable women. We have an appointment at eleven with Miss Smith and Mrs. Sheridan."

"But I only suggested having them help us a few minutes ago. How can you already have an appointment?"

"I knew what you were going to suggest, and you rose to the occasion. Come, we need to be going."

Chapter Five

Meeting at the Mayflower

olmes had arranged to meet the two women at the Mayflower Pub, a long-standing establishment that dated back to the eponymous ship and only a few blocks past the house of Lady Gwendolyn Ottoline Carrington. On a weekday, however, it was nearly an hour away from Baker Street. But it was a pleasant summer morning, and I enjoyed the ride that took us first to the Embankment and then along the Thames to the recently completed magnificent Tower Bridge.

As we traveled, I took a long look at Sherlock Holmes. From time to time, I had asked myself what it was, after nearly twenty years, that compelled me to leap out of bed and scramble to follow this unusual man. The easy answer was the thrill of the chase. What military man does not find his heart racing as he charges into battle, knowing that his life may be in danger, but assured that he is fighting on the side of justice? The more accurate answer, I had to admit, was the irresistible hold this man had on me. Having observed him closely for so many years, I knew that with his brilliance and drive, he could have been a member of Cabinet, or a captain of industry, or a major general. Yet he chose to forego all those esteemed roles and dedicate himself to bringing solace to the victims of crime by the relentless pursuit of clever but vile criminals and dragging them before a judge.

I smiled at him, and once again considered myself oddly blessed.

As we came into Rotherhithe, I looked at my watch and was puzzled.

"Holmes," I said, "the pub will not be open yet."

"I sent a note to the publican asking him to allow us to meet there. I offered to pay him with a signed copy of one of the books you wrote about me. Books signed by the author are considered to have a higher status."

"But you were not the author. I was."

"Let us not quibble over details."

The Mayflower Pub was a small, Thames-side establishment that was filled with paraphernalia related to the American Pilgrims and their historic voyage. It was festooned inside with the Stars and Stripes, prints of Washington crossing the Delaware and other scenes of the colony that got away. At an hour before opening, it still smelled of the stale beer, sweat and other bodily odors from the previous night that one is used to being assaulted by in any English pub before the cleaning staff has completed their morning chores.

Looking through the pub, I could see the wooden deck and tables that abutted the river. Two women were sitting at one of the tables. We walked toward them but paused at the bar. Mr. Frank Farber, the inspector on loan from the MMP was seated there, and he waved a hand in greeting to us.

I whispered to Holmes. "What is he doing here?"

"It was not my idea," he muttered back. "Lestrade insisted, and he is paying the piper."

Sherlock Holmes might not have appreciated the intrusion of the man from the Mounted Military Police, but I rather liked the chap and I sauntered over and we greeted each other. Having done so, we followed Holmes out to the back deck and sat down at the table occupied by the two women.

The setting of our meeting struck me as somewhat incongruous. It was as ideal a day as anyone can hope for in England. The sun was shining and a light breeze wafted across the River Thames, bringing with it the intermingled smell of the water and the whiffs of smoke and steam that belched from the passing barges and ships. And here we were, about to talk about a vile murder and try to identify whoever it was, posing amongst the literary establishment of London, who was also an indiscriminate killer.

Mrs. Sheridan acknowledged our greeting in a cool, perfunctory way, but Miss Smith was more pleasant and, for a second, she flashed a warm smile toward me. I could not help but notice that she had regained her color and, with her hair all in place and just a light touch of cosmetics, she was once again the very attractive woman I remembered from two decades ago. Of course, she was twenty years older, but then, so was I.

Holmes has little use for idle chit-chat but was decent enough to extend his condolences and to note his understanding of the effect that the death of Lady Carrington had on the lives of these two women.

"I do appreciate," he said, "the immediate need both of you have to find an alternative situation. You have been dependent on Her Ladyship for your financial sustenance and now must find means of replacing it. It is, I am sure, a matter of some urgency for you, and I am grateful for your setting aside time to meet with us. We need your help in sorting out what happened."

Miss Smith quietly acknowledged his remarks, but Mrs. Sheridan gave him a hard look.

"Your assumption, as it pertains to me, Mr. Holmes, is false."

"Madam?"

For several seconds she just sat and glared at him. I noted that she was not dressed in the nurse's uniform we had seen her in the day before but wore an elegant charcoal skirt, a fine linen blouse, and a jacket that might have come from one of the better shops on Bond Street.

"I have not been dependent on Lady Gwendolyn for income. I have been dependent on her for mental stimulation."

"Kindly explain."

"I am not only a certified nurse. I have studied additional aspects of medicine and business. My four children flew from the nest some years ago, and I am now blessed with seven grandchildren. I visit with them every Sunday, and that is more than enough. My husband, to whom I was happily married for forty-one years, passed away eight years ago. I was left with more than enough income to live on and am the sole owner of a valuable home a few doors down from that of Lady Gwendolyn. After I was widowed, what I became was utterly bored. I met my neighbor through our dogs. I have a black Labrador retriever, Maggie, who became friendly with her spaniel, Pilot, six years ago when both of them were still young enough to take an unwanted interest in each other. Lady Gwen and I chatted, and she told me about her need for assistance running her household and her personal affairs, and I agreed to help her. I assured her that I could supervise her staff and make certain that not a single speck of dust would ever be out of order. She hired me on the spot. It has been fascinating work and allowed me to meet some very interesting, even if not altogether likable or admirable, people. I shall miss all of them. They were, shall we say, *unusual*."

"How interesting, madam," said Holmes. "It is about six of these unusual people that we are in need of your insights."

"What do you want to know?"

"I shall defer to Inspector Farber to begin our questions. Will you take it from here, Inspector?"

The look of surprise on Inspector Farber said that he was not expecting that. Neither was I. I wondered if Holmes was engaging in a subtle skirmish and letting it be known that he was not pleased with having Scotland Yard hovering over him as he worked.

To his credit, the inspector immediately recovered and proceeded.

"Thank you, Mr. Holmes, I shall do so. Forgive me if I seem less than adequately imaginative. We in the military are required to go by the book, and the book always starts with *cui bono*. So, perhaps one or both of you two ladies could please tell me who becomes the beneficiary of Lady Carrington's estate? Who ends up with her money and other assets?"

He looked first at Mrs. Sheridan.

"Unless a Will is found," she said, "and I have never heard her mention one, it all goes to her next of kin. As she had no children, I assume that everything will go to her next closest relative, and that is her step-brother, Mr. Clive Merryweather Clapper."

"Do you have any idea how much the estate is worth?"

"She owns over two thousand acres in Cornwall from which the rents are very lucrative, and two tin mines. There is a manor house that is the ancestral home, which she owns. She was a very wealthy woman."

"Was she now? And what about this journal she published? What happens to it?"

"That is part of her estate, and so it will also go to Clive."

"Is that your understanding as well, Miss Smith?" Inspector Farber asked, turning to the younger woman.

"No. I do not wish to contradict Mrs. Sheridan, who knows far more than I do about Her Ladyship's personal affairs. However, she told me in passing not long ago that in the event of her death—she imagined herself either drowning at sea or being hanged for treason; she had a somewhat exaggerated imagination when it came to her own demise—she had established a trust for the *Review* and attached it as a codicil to her Will. I have never seen it, but that is what she said."

"And who, if you do not mind my asking, was to be in control of the trust?"

"I assume her executor."

"And do you know who that was?"

"No, I'm sorry, I don't, but perhaps Mrs. Sheridan does."

All eyes now turned to the older woman.

"If there is a Will," she said, "it would be my guess that she named Lady Mary Williams."

The questions paused. A minute later, Holmes responded.

"What, may I ask, is the reason for your guess?"

"The two of them," said Mrs. Sheridan, "have known each other all their lives."

"Ah, so they must have trusted each other," said Holmes.

"They must have," said Miss Smith, "but I can think of no reason why."

Chapter Six

Dinner at Simpson's

olmes ignored Millie's snide comment and pressed on.

"Thank you, Inspector. Knowing who benefited from her death is useful. What I now wish to know is who amongst those who were at the soirée had an animus toward her. Who hated her enough to want to kill her, even if it meant killing others at the same time?"

Mrs. Sheridan shook her head. "No one. They were self-centered, vengeful, and petty. But none of them was given to violence. They were, as Miss Smith told you when you came to the house, *writers*. They wrote about horrible murders, even multiple murders. But they did not commit them."

Holmes now turned to Miss Smith. "Are you of the same opinion, Miss?"

"Yes…well…I don't know. They were all angry with her at one time or the other. The most recent was Thoby MacCarthy. I did not mind him, but he was horrid to her. But to murder her? I really don't think he was capable of it."

"Why was he horrid?"

"His satirical essays and short fiction had savaged a few too many people who hold power over all of the arts."

"The critics?"

"Oh, goodness, no. She considered all of the Press to be flies swarming toward any recent pile of manure. No, Mr. MacCarthy had offended too many of those people who have the money to control the art galleries, the museums, the serious theaters, and the orchestras. No matter how fine a journal we assembled and published, they could put us out of business by having us banned by all the printers and the bookstores and censored by any number of government officials. So, she could not afford to accept any more of his work."

"But could he not go to another magazine?" Holmes asked, "One that had no illusions of decency and quality? There are a dozen or more of those on the racks all the time."

"No. She had him under contract and paid him a monthly stipend regardless of whether or not she accepted anything he wrote. That was what he lived on, and he lived well, if you judge by the size of him."

"Had they argued?"

"They had had words, often. He was very angry with her. He thought of himself as an artist, and he would not tolerate anyone telling him what he could and could not write."

"Angry enough to kill?" asked Holmes.

"I would not want to think so, but Caravaggio was an artist, wasn't he?"

Holmes and Inspector Farber asked several more questions, but no further insights were given. We thanked the women, departed, and walked a block away to another pub where we ate a quick lunch.

"Your suggestions, gentlemen," Holmes said to the two of us.

"If you will permit me, Mr. Holmes," said the inspector. "If this were my case, I would start at the top of the list and move immediately to interview the brother and the fat satirist."

"An excellent suggestion, sir, and that is what we shall do."

Our food was served, and then, to the inspector's surprise, although not to mine, Holmes retreated into silence. He ate his fish and chips and mushy peas slowly without looking at his plate more than was necessary to know where to aim his fork. Inspector Farber tried to engage him several times in conversation, but Holmes rudely ignored him and did not so much as look up. Before any of us had finished, Holmes abruptly stood up.

"Good day, gentlemen. I have to go. I shall send you instructions concerning when and where we shall meet tomorrow."

He walked out of the pub, leaving the inspector open-mouthed and me shrugging.

"Is he always so strange," asked Farber. "That was positively rude."

"Oh no," I said. "There are many days when he is much worse."

With Holmes gone, the two of us were free to do what all veterans love to do. We swapped war stories.

It was just as well that Holmes vanished until the following day, as I had my own plans for the evening, and they most certainly did not include him.

By half-past six, I had bathed and shaved and was dressed. I had not chosen typical evening dress. Instead, I left my linen shirt open at the collar and covered the hairs of my chest with a bright yellow cravat of Italian silk. I pulled on a short, dark blazer, cut in the American style, and wore my finest, tooled-leather boots.

At five minutes to seven, my cab let me out at Simpson's-in-the-Strand, and I waited at the door. On the stroke of seven, another cab pulled up, and Miss Mildred Smith stepped out. She was wearing a long, loose black cotton dress with red flowers scattered across it. Ringlets of hair dangled and swayed in front of her ears, which were accentuated with her only jewelry, large golden hoop earrings. As she walked toward me, the wind blew her dress against her long legs causing me to gasp quietly.

I gave her my arm and led her into the magnificent dark-paneled dining room.

"Oh, John," she said, "this was so thoughtful of you. It is exactly what I needed after the past horrible two days. Thank you."

A waiter led us to our table, and I allowed myself a moment to enjoy the stares of the seated patrons. I thought that we were quite the dashing couple, even if no longer all that young.

In keeping with the instructions I had sent on ahead, as soon as we were seated, a waiter appeared with two flutes of chilled Champagne.

I raised my glass. "To catching up on the past two decades."

She raised hers in return. "And to never letting so many years go by again."

We chatted amiably over an excellent bottle of French wine and Simpson's famous roast beef on the trolley, carved at our table. She told me about her work, beginning with when she helped Lady Gwendolyn get *The Cornwall Monthly Review* started and watching it grow into one of the most highly praised literary journals of the day. I told her all about my adventures with Sherlock Holmes. Each of us had amusing anecdotes to relate and, encouraged by the wine, we laughed heartily.

When the main course had been cleared away, she looked directly into my eyes. "I read about your loss of Mary, John. I'm so sorry for that. You must miss her terribly."

I was a bit taken aback, but composed myself and replied. "It was very hard at the time. But that was several years ago now, and I have my writing, my medical practice, and my escapades with Sherlock Holmes to fill my every waking minute. So, I manage fairly well these days."

"Oh, John, you are such a writer."

"What? What do you mean, I am such a *writer*?"

"I work with writers every day. You make things up and pretend they are true. You are all liars."

"Really, Millie—"

"Oh, John. I can see it all over you. You miss being loved and in love. You miss falling asleep and waking up with the one to whom you have given your heart. Sherlock Holmes is a useful bandage on your soul, but he has not stopped the bleeding."

I was about to offer some witty repartee, but the words did not appear. I suddenly felt myself becoming rather emotional and struggled not to let it show in my eyes. I got a hold of myself and replied.

"You may be right, Millie. But he has become my life, and I am grateful for him. He really is something. But what about you, my dear? You never married?"

"Never. Well, you could say that I married my work, my passion. I cannot write worth a tuppence, but I can take some rough piece of fiction, or an essay, or a poem that someone with some degree of talent has drafted and by cutting, and rearranging, and correcting and polishing, I can make it shine. Those gems I included in each issue of our *Review.* I put my heart and soul into it every month. That is what I do and have done every day for twenty years."

"Ah, but maybe a gentleman or two might have stolen your heart in between monthly issues?"

"Oh, yes, several…well… more than several, but none that I kept for more than a year."

"Too dull? Too much a stuffed shirt? Too overweight? Too old?"

"No, none of those. Most were brilliant. Accomplished. Charming. Even handsome."

"Then why?"

"I suppose I would have to say … oh dear … this is not going to come out well … they were just too *married.*"

I felt my mouth falling open. I was utterly speechless. She looked at me and broke out in a peal of laughter.

"Oh, John. I'm sorry. I did not want to spoil a lovely dinner. It is just that the crowd I had been part of—the writers, the painters, the opera singers, the whole lot of us—we all like to pretend that we have true bohemian souls. We are liberated. What was it some American woman said about us? We live in squares, write in circles, and love in triangles."

"But … but if a man is married, he can never truly become the partner of your soul."

"And that is why they are so safe, my dear. If they were available, I would run the risk of falling in love and what a disaster that would be. I could never think clearly about my work again."

I said nothing and took a slow sip of my wine. Then I looked directly into her eyes.

"Millie, I am not married."

"I know John, and that is why you are a very dangerous man."

"Danger, my dear, is highly addictive. I can assure you of that. Why do you think I go running all over England with Sherlock Holmes?"

"And why do you think I accepted your invitation to dinner?"

I felt my heart starting to race and noticed a tiny tremble in my hands. I changed the subject.

"Ah, yes, well, speaking of Sherlock Holmes. He appreciated the insights you gave him this morning."

"Did he now? Well then, I am going to ask him to return the favor."

"Oh, how?"

"Someone murdered Gwendolyn, and that same someone tried to murder me. I took exception to it. So, I am going to drop my beloved reading and editing for however long it takes to find out who it was. I am going to join you and Sherlock Holmes and use whatever skills I have, and *we* are going to work together. We are going to solve the mystery. We are going to find the villain and see that justice is done. Will you please convey my decision to Mr. Holmes?"

"Oh, yes, certainly. I must say, this could become quite … quite, well, *interesting.*"

"What you mean to say, John, if you will allow me to exercise my expertise as an editor, is that it could become *dangerous.*"

I reached for my wine.

"And John," she said, after both of us had consumed several more sips, "I do hope I am not being presumptuous, but I am assuming that with your asking me for dinner and such a lovely time together, that you are willing to let bygones be bygones."

"Any unpleasantness of twenty years ago," I said, "is water under the bridge. Much better to remember the good times of the past and look forward to more of the same in the future."

I raised my glass, and she responded in kind.

We made it through dessert by retreating to safer topics of conversation such as politics and religion. When dinner was over, we walked out to the Strand, and I hailed a cab. It was a perfect summer evening, and I was not eager to have it end.

"Might I have the honor," I said, "of seeing you to your home?"

"No, my dear. It is exactly the wrong direction for you. I live to the east and you to the west."

"I really do not mind."

"Next time," she said and then moved toward me and gave me a kiss … on my lips.

Again, I was speechless, and she laughed gaily.

"Can you not see my villainous ways? I want to be sure that there *is* a next time. Good night, John. Pleasant dreams and please, not about Sherlock Holmes."

I walked back to Baker Street, about six inches above the ground the entire way.

When I returned to the front room, I went over to where Pilot was stretched out and picked him up.

"Did you have an enjoyable evening, old fellow? I certainly did. Let me tell you about it."

I sat down, with a spaniel curled up in my lap, and I told him a lovely story.

Chapter Seven

Unwelcomed by Mr. Clapper

I woke early the following morning, having enjoyed some pleasant dreams and I made my way down from my bedroom. An old dog with a wriggling backend greeted me and barked happily after I found him something to eat.

Holmes was already up and gone and had left me a note on the breakfast table. I picked it up and then stopped. Directly underneath it was a small envelope bearing my name and address, written in an elegant, feminine hand. I opened it first and read:

My dear John:

Were I to fill this entire page with words, I could not begin to express the serenity that bathed my soul after our wonderful time together. After the horror of Lady Carrington's murder and the terror of knowing that I was almost murdered, your calm, gentlemanly company brought peace to my heart. I know it has been many years, but I confess, as I sat and looked on your kindly face, it was as if those years had vanished and we had picked up where we left off so long ago. And please, my dear John, permit a further confession. I buy and read every copy of the Strand magazine when your stories about Sherlock Holmes appear. You truly are an inspired writer and, if I may be less than modest, I am one of England's most demanding and discerning judges. I so look forward to seeing you again. I hope and pray it will be soon. I remain, Yours very truly,

It was signed by 'Millie.'

I read it again ... and again. I might have sat down and enjoyed it countless times, but the note from Holmes also demanded my attention and wrenched me out of my reverie. It ran:

Meeting arranged this a.m. with Clapper. Afternoon with MacCarthy. Be prepared to depart at 9:00. Farber will join us. No need for service revolver. Holmes.

Over the generous breakfast Mrs. Hudson provided, I re-read Millie's letter one more time before putting it down and preparing for my day with Holmes. At fifteen minutes to nine, the bell on Baker Street rang, and Inspector Frank Farber came up the stairs to join me. I offered him a cup of coffee, and he asked me if I had any idea what Holmes was thinking.

"None whatsoever. Do you?"

"I'm in as thick a fog as you are, Doctor. Is he always like this?"

"Oh, no. Sometimes he disappears for days."

We enjoyed our coffee and chatted about football until interrupted on the stroke of nine by the arrival of Sherlock Holmes.

"Come, please, gentlemen. I have a cab waiting."

"Mind telling us where we are going?" I asked.

"Fitzrovia. Clive Clapper lives on Cleveland Street."

The old spaniel whimpered when he realized I was not going to take him with me, but I was now on duty with Sherlock Holmes. I was anxious not only to pepper him with questions but also to inform him of Mildred Smith's insistence that she help with the investigation. Once we were inside the cab, he waved off anything I tried to say, opened his small valise, and extracted material he was intent on examining.

He was reading back copies of the *Cornwall Monthly Review*.

As we pulled into an address just north of the intersection of Cleveland with Goodge and Newman, he put the journals back in his valise and muttered.

"For the life of me, I cannot understand how it is that writers who make themselves utterly incomprehensible are considered to be *artistes*. Most of what I have read is beyond the pale. Did you know, Watson, that there is a woman who writes murder mysteries—yes, murder mysteries!—who makes them impossible to understand? At least your stories are simple enough that any schoolboy or chambermaid can follow. And she is considered a *sophisticated literary talent*. Balderdash."

Speaking of literary talent, the house we had stopped at was, I recognized, one in which Charles Dickens had lived in the early years of his career. It had to be the prettiest house on the block with an azure blue door and window frames, recent whitewash, and flower boxes overflowing with geraniums.

"Is this where Clive Clapper lives?" I asked.

"It is," said Holmes.

"I wonder," I said, "if he deliberately chose to live in the same place as Dickens once did? Perhaps he imagined the spirit of Boz would rub off."

"I suspect," said Holmes, "that his motives were much more related to such pretense as is required of a *poseur.*"

"Really, Holmes. We have no idea what he is like."

"No? Well then, come and meet him and see if you agree with me."

We knocked on the door and, after we waited for several minutes and knocked twice more, it opened. The man who greeted us was dressed in tight trousers and a white linen shirt that was open at the neck and augmented by a bright yellow cravat of Italian silk. His boots were finely tooled and gleaming. For a moment, I was nonplussed until I noted that, unlike my habit of the previous evening, the sleeves of his arms were wide and flowing, and his trousers were tucked into the boots. For a fleeting instant, I imagined that he could easily tie a sash around his waist and secure employment as a waiter at Goldini's.

"Good morning, sir. My name is Sherlock Holmes—"

"Oh, my gaawd," he said and rolled his eyes, "the amateur detective himself. Do the world a favor, Mr. Holmes, and go away. I am frightfully busy and have neither the time nor the interest in talking to you."

He started to close the door in Holmes's face when an anguished voice cried out from behind him.

"Daaaddy, it's Sherlock Holmes. Let him in."

While still blocking the doorway, he turned around to face an adolescent girl who had entered the vestibule and was standing, glaring at him, her hands firmly on her hips.

"Felicity, this does not concern you. Please—"

"Of course, it concerns me, Daddy. Sherlock Holmes is marvelously famous, and he is here at my house. And...oh my goodness...is that Dr. Watson too?"

She deftly squirmed her way in front of her father and gave a short bow to Holmes and then spoke to me.

"Dr. Watson, it is such an honor. I so adore your stories. Please, gentlemen, do come in. I am sure my father would be thrilled to chat with you. Wouldn't you, Daddy."

Mr. Clapper emitted an exasperated sigh and stepped aside and allowed us to enter the house.

His daughter was tall and lithe for her age and blessed with long blonde hair that cascaded down over her shoulders. She was wearing her school uniform, and the thought occurred to me that she had hiked her kilt up several inches above the regulation length. As we entered the house, she approached me.

"Oh, Dr. Watson, I shall be so proud to tell the girls in my class that you came to my home. They will be so jealous. We all find your stories so utterly fascinating. Please be seated. I have so many questions to ask you."

"Young lady," said Inspector Farber, rather severely. "I am Inspector Farber of Scotland Yard. We are here on a police matter, and you will have to arrange another time to pose your questions to Dr. Watson."

"But—"

"No buts, young lady. I thank you for inviting us in, but I am telling you that you will now have to leave and go to your room so we can have a confidential conversation with your father."

"But—"

"Now. And you do not argue with a police officer."

With a look of haughty indignation, followed by a heart-breaking pout, she departed, and I heard her ascending the stairs. I could not say for certain, but it sounded as if she stopped before reaching the top and sat down.

"As you can see," said Clapper, "the gods are just and of our pleasant nights of vice over a decade ago, send instruments to plague us. If I must have you in my home, come into the parlor. Do not sit down until I have covered the chairs with towels. There is no telling where your arses have been recently."

He vanished and returned bearing three clean dish towels that he spread on the chairs to which he had directed us. He sat down with his back straight, put his hands in his lap, and crossed his legs. I glanced around the room and noted some original paintings and several prints by the American artist, Thomas Eakins, and the French fellow, Paul Gaugin. All of them depicted young men and women in various stages of *déshabillé* and *au naturel.* About the mantel was a large photograph of Oscar Wilde, taken when he was young and handsome and well before his recent incarceration. Perhaps I was somewhat old-fashioned in my beliefs about an appropriate setting in which to raise an impressionable child, but this certainly was not it.

Once the three of us were seated, Inspector Farber continued in his authoritative voice.

"Please confirm whether or not you attended a soirée the night before last at the home of Lady Carrington."

"Oh, puhleese. You would not be here if you did not already know that I did. And so was my daughter, which you know as well. Next question, and do try to make it more intelligent than your first."

"What time did you arrive?"

"Half-past seven. Next."

"Can you tell us the names of the others who were present during the last hour of the event?"

"Good gawd. They are whomever you already have on your list. Next."

"I asked you a question, Mr. Clapper. Please answer it. If you choose not to, we can continue at Scotland Yard Headquarters."

"Oh, very well. If you are that touchy about it. Well then, let me think about that one."

He closed his eyes and tilted his head toward the ceiling. Slowly and dramatically, he counted on the fingers of his left hand, switched hands and continued on his right, and concluded back on his left.

"There were ten of us: the simple young maid, but she left immediately after she had put out the food; Gwen's hired guns, Mildred and Mrs. Sheridan; as well as Thoby, Saxon, Ouinon, Reverend Eddie, Lady Mary, Gwendolyn and me. Does that make ten? Eleven if you count Felicity. Let me count again."

"That will not be necessary. What time did you leave?"

"Did Mrs. Sheridan not already tell you? I'm sure she could if you asked her. I left at twenty-five minutes past ten."

Inspector Farber checked off items in a notebook with each answer.

"Thank you, sir," he continued. "Now then, what was your relationship to Lady Carrington?"

"My relationship? I suppose you could say she was my patroness and publisher. She paid me well for the stories I wrote, and which she printed in her *Review.*"

"What was your familial relationship to her?"

"Oh, my. You boys have been doing your homework, haven't you? She was my step-sister. She was our father's legitimate offspring. But five years later, Daddy decided that her governess was more interesting than his wife, and along I came. Yes, I was Edmund to her Edgar. *I grow; I prosper: Now, gods, stand up for bastards!* Next question."

The inspector looked over at Holmes. "Carry on, please, Mr. Holmes."

"What is the value," he said, "of the estate and assets you will now inherit?"

"Oh, good lord, I assure you, sir, I have no idea."

"I assure you, sir, I do not believe you. Please answer my question."

That brought an angry glare from Mr. Clapper.

"Frankly, Mr. Detective, I do not wish to waste my time with such trivial matters."

"And I am too busy to waste one second believing you. But I will keep on wasting both your time and mine asking the question until you answer it. What is the value?"

"I suppose it is approximately—"

"The precise value," said Holmes.

"Well, aren't you the picky one. Fine. As of the end of the first quarter of this year, the rents were three-thousand, two hundred and twenty pounds a year. The property was evaluated by an estate agent in December at nine-thousand, nine hundred and ninety pounds. That, mind you, was the value he gave with the hope of being enlisted to put it up for sale, so who knows."

"Thank you. Now, the value of cash and securities."

"Are you familiar with the stock market, Mr. Holmes? If you are, then you will not make a foolish demand of a precise value. The worth of the stocks and bonds in the Carrington portfolio may have changed since we sat down."

"Approximate value within one hundred pounds will be acceptable," said Holmes.

"About five hundred."

Holmes paused and raised his eyebrows. "That is less than I had expected. However, you are about to become a wealthy man."

"Yes, Mr. Holmes. My sister was not only rich, she was something that rhymes with rich."

"So be it. Let us carry on. The value of the *Cornwall Monthly Review*?"

"Zero. *Rien. Nada. Waardeloos.* Nugatory."

Holmes gave Clapper a puzzled look and received a smug smirk in return.

"The *Review*," said Holmes, "has the highest circulation of any literary journal in the country. How can you say it has no value?"

"It seems that your ignorance extends to the world of publishing, Mr. Holmes. Perhaps your doctor friend can enlighten you. I will save him the trouble. Literary reviews take years to pay for themselves and cannot survive long without a wealthy patron or two. *Cornwall* lost money for years, and Gwendolyn kept bailing it out. After twenty years, it is now turning a handsome profit, buy it will not be worth a *sou* unless Miss Mildred-the-Kill-dread agrees to carry on as editor."

"Explain, please."

"I would have thought it was self-explanatory. But since you require an explanation, let me offer you one in simple enough terms for you to understand. Gwendolyn had the ambition and the money and not an ounce of talent. But the rich can always buy brains, and she bought Mildred Smith. She was the editor who turned our little magazine into a gem. She routinely savaged our submissions, murdered them mercilessly, and turned them from mediocre into marvelous. If she can be persuaded to carry on, the *Review* will carry on. If not, it will die."

"And will she?"

"No one knows. She has no other life, but I will be the new owner, and she is not particularly fond of me, and the feeling is mutual. Although, I am told that there is an entire trunk full of manuscripts ready and waiting to be published. But their existence is only rumored and any value impossible to assess."

"Thank you for your explanation. Mr. Clapper. Now then—"

"If you are thinking, Mr. Holmes, that I murdered my sister for the vast amounts of money I will now receive, let me explain something else to you."

"Proceed."

"I already have a decent living and need no more income to enjoy my life and provide for my daughter. I will devote every farthing I inherit from Gwendolyn to setting up a trust for young writers. It will be in honor of the most brilliant talent to have graced our minds for the past quarter-century."

He gestured theatrically to the portrait of Oscar Wilde.

"I will," he said, "establish the Oscar Wilde Trust for young authors, the earnest ones. You may quote me on that. Felicity will help. I will be paying a visit to a solicitor in the Inner Temple tomorrow. Do you want to know his name so you can go and play detective, Mr. Holmes?"

"That will not be necessary. Allow me a final question, Mr. Clapper. Are you aware that your sister gave instructions that a major portion of her estate be placed in a trust and the proceeds used for the continued operation of the *Cornwall Monthly Review?*"

This question elicited a smirk from Clapper. "Allow me, Mr. Holmes, to ask you a question. Have you seen any document which in writing and signed by my sister that authenticates such a request? ... Mr. Holmes? ... Answer my question, Mr. Holmes. Have you?"

"I have not."

"I didn't think so. Neither have I."

Holmes concluded the interview, and we rose and departed the parlor.

"Mr. Holmes," called a voice from the top of the stairs, "do you not want to question me too? I was there, you know."

Miss Clapper descended from her listening post and came and stood directly in front of Holmes.

"Felicity!" said her father. "Get back up—"

"No, Mr. Clapper," said Inspector Farber. "This is a murder investigation, and if Mr. Holmes wishes to ask questions of your daughter, he is entitled to do so. You may demand to have a solicitor present if you wish."

"Good heavens, inasmuch as I despise lawyers, I cannot think of one who I hate so much as to foist my daughter on him. Go ahead, Holmes."

He gave us a haughty look, turned and strutted down the hallway. The pout was familiar.

"Well then, Miss," said Holmes, "can you confirm that you were present at Lady Carrington's soirée for the entire event."

"I was, but you already knew that, didn't you, Mr. Holmes?"

"I had already been *told* that, but that does not mean I knew it to be true. You might want to remember that as you grow up. And why were you there? You are old enough to be left home alone and still several years from belonging in an event for adults."

If the girl was offended by Holmes's dismissive comment, she did not show it.

"I was invited to attend and to read one of my poems. It has been said that my poetry reminds sophisticated readers of the poetry of Charles Algernon Swinburne. Would you like me to recite it for you?"

"No. Did Lady Carrington invite you?" asked Holmes.

Miss Felicity was looking altogether put out by Holmes decided lack of interest in her work, but she answered his question nonetheless.

"No, Mr. Holmes. She has little or nothing to do with the programs of her *soirées*. Miss Smith looks after that, and she invited me."

"You stayed until the very end, though. What did you do after you read your poem?"

"I sat in a chair in the corner and pretended to write another poem. I have been working on one that is inspired by Robert Browning. I am really absolutely fond of him."

"What do you mean, you pretended?"

"In truth, I was listening to what everyone was chatting about. It is an excellent way to acquire dialogue and content for my stories. I also write murder mysteries."

"I am sure they make amusing fiction. What of any significance did you overhear whilst eavesdropping?"

"I would have to say that everyone spoke highly of Lady Carrington's food and beverages, and no one spoke highly of her. They all find her ... shall I say, rebarbative. But everyone admires Miss Mildred Smith—she has been my teacher—although some refer to her as General Mildred or, well, there are those like my father who call her something utterly nasty and not-at-all flattering and most undeserved."

"And you made notes of who said what to whom."

"I did. Shall I show them to you?"

"No."

That reply also took her by surprise and appeared to hurt her feelings. I was afraid she was about to break into tears and I intervened.

"I would very much like to see them," I said. "And if you are willing to let me read your murder mysteries, I would be most appreciative."

She lit up like a sunrise. "Oh, yes, of course, Dr. Watson. That would be utterly splendid."

Once the three of us were standing on the pavement of Cleveland Street, I chastised both Holmes and Inspector Farber for the way they spoke to the young woman.

"I did nothing other," said the inspector, "than speak to her the way I do to a new private."

"She is a young girl," I said, "not a soldier."

"True, but young soldiers away from home for the first time are as child-like in their feelings as a fifteen-year-old girl. They both need a firm hand."

"Enough of her," said Holmes. "What did you think of her father."

"Can't say as I liked him," said the inspector. "Mind you, for the past decade, I have had contact only with members of Her Majesty's armed forces. Not a man in the BEF would be caught dead wearing a flowing white shirt with a sissified yellow silk cravat."

I made no comment.

"As for me," said Holmes, "I have yet to meet a man so devoted to a noble cause that he would completely give up such a vast fortune. I shall believe it only when I see it, and I doubt I will. But enough of Mr. Clapper. We now move on to the writer who appears to have utterly hated Lady Carrington."

Chapter Eight

Mr. MacCarthy Regrets

r. Thoby MacCarthy lived in Bermondsey, a few blocks south of Lady Carrington's, just off Jamaica Road. His house was one of those substantial erratics of red brick that, by forces unknown, ended up sandwiched between whitewashed terraced homes of more modest construction. At one o'clock in the afternoon, we knocked on the door. A young maid opened it and stared at us in surprise.

"Oh ... oh, we had not expected you so soon. But ... but please do come in and...and make yourselves comfortable in the parlor. The ladies will be right with you."

We looked at each other and followed her. Once seated, I turned to Holmes. "Did she say they expected us? Did you tell Mr. MacCarthy that we were coming?"

"No. And yes, it is odd."

We sat for ten minutes, and then the maid reappeared, bearing a tray with tea for three and some pieces of shortbread.

"I am so sorry to make you wait, gentlemen. Miss MacCarthy and Mrs. Grant will be with you momentarily. They apologize for not being ready for callers so soon."

She departed, and again we looked at each other.

Five minutes later, two women entered the room. Both were slender and, even without a spot of cosmetics, rather attractive. Oddly they were both dressed entirely in black.

"Good afternoon, gentlemen. Thank you so much for coming to pay your respects. We did not print a notice as we did not want our brother's enemies, and he had so many of them, coming and dancing on his grave."

Merciful heavens. The man is dead. This thought occurred to the three of us simultaneously, and we stole glances at each other.

"We are Thoby MacCarthy's sisters," said the younger of them. "I am Virginia Grant, and my sister is Vanessa MacCarthy. Would you be so kind as to sign the book of condolences?"

She set a leather-bound book on the coffee table in front of us, along with a pen and ink well. There was nothing else we could do, and all three signed our names.

"Oh, my goodness," said Mrs. Grant. "Are you Sherlock Holmes and Dr. Watson?"

We nodded and mumbled in the affirmative.

"I would never have guessed," she said, "that Thoby would have been friends with the two of you. Oh my, he was just full of surprises. I can't wait to tell my sons that their Uncle Thoby was friends with Sherlock Holmes. They will be tickled."

Holmes seemed to have recovered his equanimity, smiled graciously at her comment, and asked the irresistible question in as tangential way as possible.

"As there was no notice posted of his passing, we only learned through the grapevine. As a result, we are entirely in a fog as to what happened to him. I hope you don't mind our asking. He seemed so alive only a few days ago."

"Oh, yes, wasn't he? Always overflowing with life and laughter. But with his heart being the way it was, we all knew he could go any day. When you are over twenty-five stone for twenty years, you cannot expect your heart to last very long. We all tried to get him to lose weight, but there was not a chance of that happening. We have to be thankful for the years he spent with us."

"My condolences for your loss," said Holmes. "I expect you will miss him terribly."

"We shall indeed," said Vanessa MacCarthy. "We shall miss sitting around the table and laughing uncontrollably at what he had written that skewered some lord or politician. The public thought he was hilarious, but they only read the pieces he toned down. We would be weeping with laughter and telling him, 'You can't print that,' and he would have to take the truly outrageous parts out."

"Again, forgive me," said Holmes, "but when precisely did he pass away? We heard no details at all."

"He came home on Sunday evening," said Miss MacCarthy, "from another one of Lady Carrington's events and said he was not feeling well. He blamed it on the rich food he ate, and he ate far too much of it. He always did. He went up to bed and went to sleep. In the middle of the night, about two o'clock, he got up and was quite ill. He went back to bed and did not wake up. The maid found him in the morning."

"I am so sorry to hear about him," said Holmes. "You say he attended other events at Lady Carrington's. I gather she published many of his satirical articles. Were he and Lady Carrington good friends?"

This question brought spontaneous laughter from the two women.

"Oh, my goodness, no," sputtered Mrs. Grant. "She was always angry at him."

"Ah, yes, that makes sense. He did get a bit carried away, making fun of the high and mighty."

"Oh, no. It wasn't that. She loved the articles he wrote about politicians and other writers, and the aristocracy. But he kept sending her articles that made fun of *her*. He had a wicked sense of humor. He would read us something he wrote about her and ask if we thought it would send the wind up her backside. He thought she was the most pretentious hypocrite in all of London. Maybe we should not say that he disliked her. It would be more accurate to say that he despised her. He merely saw her as fair game, and it made her furious."

"Oh, I see. Yes. And just one last question about him, if I may. Were you aware that Lady Carrington passed away on Sunday night as well?"

The look of shock on their faces made it clear that they were not.

"We have not been out of the house since Thoby died," said Miss MacCarthy. "What with the calls from his solicitor and the funeral director. No. Oh my. That is shocking. Such a tragedy. Thoby would have had such fun mocking her all the way to her grave."

Before departing, we were shown into the dining room. An enormous casket lay on the dining room table, with a photograph of a man with oversize jowls and a wicked grin perched on top of it.

Once outside the house, Holmes reached immediately for his cigarette case and lit up.

"I believe," said Inspector Farber, "that we can strike that name off the list."

"What if," I asked, "he was murdered?"

"It is possible," said Holmes. "But to the best of my knowledge, cyanide works quickly. I shall have to make inquiries and learn if there are cases wherein it was swallowed and took four hours to take effect. Can you enlighten me, Inspector?"

"I must plead ignorance, sir. Having spent my career in the military, the murders I investigated were invariably done with guns. Soldiers prefer that method. More manly."

Chapter Nine

His Little Princess?

"Would you work for Clive Clapper?" I asked Mildred Smith as we chatted over tea at the Savoy.

Only a few hours had passed since I received her lovely note, and I was so moved that I suggested meeting again immediately. One must, I reminded myself, strike whilst the iron is hot.

"I would prefer to hang myself," she said, "but it will all depend."

"On what?"

"On what she put in her Will. I informed Mr. Holmes that Gwendolyn once told me that she had set up a trust to keep the *Review* going after she died."

"I remember your saying so. But where is the Will? If none can be found—,"

"Oh, you do not have to tell me, John. If she died intestate, it all goes to Clive. I suppose if that happens, I will have no choice. I'll have to work for him. However, if he would assign the work to his delightful daughter, and I could work only with her, it would be acceptable."

"We met her yesterday. Quite the ball of fire."

"Isn't she though? I must say, she adores me and has decided that I am a New Woman. I've helped her a few times with her stories and poems, and that was enough to have her beg me to become her guardian so she can escape from Clive. That's out of the question, but she is my little protégée."

"But if Clive Clapper does not want her to work with you, what then? Could you find another group to work for? You are now recognized as one of the finest editors in all of England."

"Thank you. That is very kind of you to say so. I suppose I could get a job at the *Strand*. But other than your wonderful stories, most of what they print belongs in the Penny Dreadfuls. However, I could, I guess, get paid to work for Clive and do nothing for an entire year while I looked for some journal that would not give me nightmares."

"How could you do that?"

"I have over one hundred submissions from our stable of writers that I have already edited and polished. They're ready to be read. But it would be so much better for me, John, if you and Mr. Holmes could find Lady Carrington's Will and prove that she wanted the trust set up."

"But then you might have to report to Lady Mary Williams."

"I could live with that. She is also from Cornwall and somewhat like Gwendolyn and somewhat not. She would not be so bad. At least she can write a sentence and put it into a coherent paragraph."

"Let us," I said, "not lose hope that we shall find the Will. Why don't you search the house again from stem to gudgeon, and Holmes and I can inquire at the Doctors' Commons or wherever Wills are registered these days."

"That would be so good of you, John," she said and smiled at me in a way that was not only warm, it was, dare I think, loving.

We chatted on over tea and absurdly small sandwiches. I had informed her of the death of Thoby MacCarthy. To my surprise, tears appeared in her dark brown eyes.

"He was," she said, "unique. The satires he wrote were scathing, but when we chatted, he was always friendly and a gentleman. I shall miss him."

We chatted about him and the questions Holmes had concerning his death. And then we chatted some more about this and that as friends do when they are not eager to part. When we finally prepared to leave, she looked directly into my eyes.

"Years ago, John, when we were friends, I never did tell you why I enjoyed your company."

"No, you didn't. May I flatter myself and believe it was that you admired my talent as a writer?"

It is not a good idea to say things to a woman that she finds hilarious whilst she is drinking tea. Mildred Smith broke out in a spontaneous guffaw, splattered her tea, and had to reach for her serviette to catch the dribbles flowing down her chin.

"Oh, good heavens, John, no. You were a hopeless writer back then. Much improved now, I must say. No, John, the reason I found myself attracted to you was because you reminded me of my father."

"Your father? He was in the army if I remember. Royal Warwickshires, wasn't he?"

"Yes, he was a veteran of several wars just as you were. You even looked a bit like him."

"And you," I said, "were his little princess?"

"No. Not at all, I was his little boy."

"His—,"

"Yes. I was his only child, and he had dreamed of having a son. So, he taught me how to kick a football, and hunt and fish, and swing a cricket bat, and even how to box according to the Marquess of Queensbury's rules. But much more than that, he read to me every evening. He read all the great books, and he not only read the stories, he would comment on the techniques of writing the author was using. He would point out the literary devices, and all the mistakes, and how a sentence could have been better written. He prepared me to enter a man's world and make my way to the top. And that is what I have done."

"And you think I am like him?"

"You are an army man who loves stories and writes them wonderfully. And on top of all that, I find you rather handsome."

She leaned over to me and planted a kiss on my lips. Then she leapt to her feet.

"Until our next time. Now, I must get back to Her Ladyship's house and start my search. I will move into the Jungle Doctor's bedroom and get to work. Please give my warm regards to Mr. Holmes."

She turned and departed the ornate foyer. I thought about running after her, but the bill had not been paid, and I did not want to be pursued by an angry waiter. I settled back and ordered a glass of Cognac.

When I returned to 221B, Holmes was sitting and reading yet another past copy of the *Cornwall Monthly Review*. He looked up at me as I entered.

"A pleasant time over tea with a brilliant and beautiful woman?" he said.

"Yes, and I suppose you are dying to tell me how you made such a clever deduction."

"There is a smile on your face and a spring in your step. You are obviously in a good mood, brought on by where you have just been."

"There are days when I come home from my surgery, and I am in a good mood."

"There are indeed. But you do not return with flecks of breadcrumbs on your suitcoat, nor with a tiny smudge of lipstick on your upper lip. And, it is difficult to tell from this distance, but there appears to be a small tea stain on your shirt. Don't tell me you had high tea and dribbled on yourself."

I looked down at my chest, harrumphed, strode to my room and changed my shirt.

"My dear Watson," said Holmes, when I returned to our front room. "Forgive me for teasing you. In truth, I am thrilled to see a glow of happiness emanating from you. Here now. Let me pour you a brandy, and you can tell me all about your conversation with Miss Smith. And spare not a single detail."

Chapter Ten

Chez Madam

"I fear I shall have to keep you busy all day today," said Holmes over breakfast the following morning. "This afternoon, we are scheduled to meet with Mr. Saxon Sydenham. But first, we have an appointment with this woman whose true name is Mary Louise Salmon, and who comes from Bury St. Edmunds. She tells people that her name is Maria Louisa de la Sauvée and that her home is in Paris. I assume that she is about as French as I am given my distant connection to Vernet."

"Where in London does she live?" I asked.

"She is a permanent guest at the Langham Hotel."

"Then she must be a lady of means."

"Perhaps. I have learned that she not only composes poems, she also writes books about young adventurous boys, most of which involve a dog."

"Oh, yes, she does indeed," I said. "She published them under the pseudonym of *Ouinon*. She's very popular. In addition to whatever

Lady Carrington paid her for her poems, she has sold thousands of books."

"Ah, so you consider her a good writer?" he said.

"No, it is just that any book that involves a dog and makes the reader cry at the end when the dog dies, is bound to sell countless copies all over the world."

"Is that so, Watson? You really must try adding one or two to your stories about me."

"I already have, but you keep shooting and poisoning them. Frankly, it's bad for sales."

He made no further comment, and we set out by Shanks' pony for the twenty minutes it took us to walk from Baker Street through Marylebone to the splendid Langham Hotel. Readers may recall that the man who could have been my father-in-law had been living there when Mary Morstan returned to London. The King of Bohemia, under the name of Count Von Kramm, had also stayed there. I made a mental note that it would be a wonderful setting in which to spend a convivial evening with Mildred Smith.

Inspector Farber was waiting for us in the lobby, and the three of us approached the front desk. The hotel manager recognized us and grinned broadly.

"Ah, Mr. Sherlock Holmes and Dr. Watson. How may we be of service to you this morning?"

I gave the name of Madam de la Sauvée, and the desk clerk called on one of his uniformed boys to take us up to her rooms. As we were about to move toward the staircase, he called me back.

"Dr. Watson, a word with you if I may."

"By all means."

"If Sherlock Holmes is meeting with this lady, perhaps he could make inquiries into her current financial situation."

"Why," I asked, "would you want him to do that?"

"Well, Doctor, it is just that she is now three months in arrears in paying her bills. She keeps on telling us that she is waiting for her royalties to come in from America and, well, Doctor, we are starting to wonder if she truly has them or if she is merely an exceptional imposter."

"She may be both. But I shall pass along your request to Mr. Holmes."

"And a word of caution. Beware of her dog. It may be small, but it can be very unpleasant."

"Her dog? Does it bite?"

"No, but it has a very nasty habit of showing its anger at guests by committing an indiscretion on their shoes."

In response to our knock on a door on the top floor of the hotel, a youngish woman opened it and greeted us.

"Ah, *Monsieur* Sherlock Holmes, and *le docteur* Watson. *Entrez, s'il vous plaît.* I had the *maître d'hôtel* send up some excellent *croissants,* Shall I pour you *une petite tasse de café*? Do you prefer *noir ou au lait*?"

As she poured us small cups of coffee, she chatted on vacantly about the food in the hotel and how it was, *bien sûr*, not what she had been raised on in France, but was really rather good for an English establishment. *Vraiment,* what could one expect these days?

The rooms were elegantly furnished in a style that I might have termed *faux Louis*. I assume that readers know to what I am referring—fussy tables and chairs that pretend to have been imported from France but were actually manufactured in Sheffield. The art on the walls was mainly prints of *en plein air* scenes by the *à la mode* school of French painters who, as far as I could tell, deliberately smudged their buildings, landscapes, haystacks and peasants. Two large *Sèvres* porcelain vases, one on each side of the room, supported bouquets of lilies, adding an exquisite fragrance to the suite.

The madam was about to say something when a tiny Yorkshire terrier came bounding into the room. He was headed straight for me, and I instinctively pulled my feet under the table to protect my shoes. My caution was not needed. The little beast must have smelled the scent of Pilot on me and barked happily, whilst wagging its minuscule tail. Then, to my shock, it leapt up into my lap and began to lick my face. I gently but firmly deposited it back onto the carpet before my trousers could be indiscreeted upon.

"*Oh la la, docteur.* My little *Patrasche* likes you. Let me tell you a wonderful story of how he came into my life. I was in *Provence* for the winter three years ago—"

"Madam," interrupted Holmes. "I am sure your story is fascinating, but it shall have to wait until another time. We need for you to give an account of a very different event."

"Ah, *c'est dommage.* But of course. You are the Auguste Dupin of London and you are investigating the murder of Lady Carrington. *Posez vos questions, Monsieur et je ferai de mon mieux pour vous répondre.*"

"At what time did you arrive at the *soirée* and when did you depart?"

"I arrived at seven and stayed until the end. I was one of the last to leave. Do you wish to know if I drank from the bottle of Port, Mr. Holmes? If I were you, I might ask that question."

That appeared to catch Holmes off-guard.

"Please tell me how you knew about the Port? That information has not been made public."

"I had a chat yesterday with Madame Sheridan, and she told me. Your next question, *s'il vous plaît.*"

"Very well then, did you consume the Port."

"*Mais oui.*, I would have much preferred to have ended the evening with a glass of *Courvoisier,* but we are in London, so what can one expect?"

"When did you drink it?"

"I poured myself a glass—the maid had already departed, and Madam Gwen was not in the habit of waiting on her guests—at fifteen minutes past ten and consumed it before departing at ten twenty-five. And as you can see, *Monsieur* Holmes, I am still *bien vivante*."

"As I can see, madam."

"*Maintenant,* you must ask me who remained in the room after I had poured my Port. Is that not *la question suivante*?"

"It is, madam. Kindly answer it."

"There was Clive, Thoby, and Mary. And your next question should be who amongst us had reason to murder Gwendolyn. And the answer to that question is *chacun de nous.*"

"Every one of you?"

"Your French is *très bon, Monsieur* Holmes. Did you study at *la Sorbonne*?"

"No madam, I acquired such facility as I have whilst conducting research in Montpellier. I assume you acquired yours, Miss Salmon, while attending a grammar school in Bury."

A flash of anger swept across her face. She stood, picked up the tray of breakfast pastries from the coffee table, and marched back toward the kitchen. A minute later, she returned and sat down.

"Right, so Mr. Sherlock Holmes has been sticking his nose into my past. Fine, what do you want to know?"

"Why *chacun de nous*?"

"Because we all chafed under the way she treated us, and we could do nothing about it. We all knew that it was Millie who was the genius behind the *Review,* but Gwen had the money and the control, and she never ceased to remind us. Mind you, there were times when every one of us would have gladly murdered Millie as well."

"And why would that be?"

"She was brutal. Two weeks after we sent any of our work to her, she politely asked us to come and meet with her. We called those meeting our invitation to the dungeon, where we would be stripped, whipped and flayed alive—metaphorically speaking—and we departed humiliated. But we knew that when our work was published, it would be praised by critics far and wide. On those days, we loved her."

"I'm sure you did. But back to my question. Who amongst those who stayed to the end of the evening might have killed Lady Carrington, and not be bothered by the possibility of also killing Mildred Smith?"

"None of us. We talked about it yesterday, and we are just not the murdering kind, Mr. Holmes. And without the *Review,* we would all be unknown scribblers, myself included, except amongst sentimentalists who weep over stories of dead dogs."

"You have had conversations with the others?"

"Indeed, I did. Several times."

"And who then do you—plural—suspect?"

"Right. That should have been your question at the start. *We* think you should be giving a good look to *le grand docteur blanc,* Bwana Sterndale. You do know, don't you, that he was in London that night, and the night before."

"I do know that. But how do you?"

"Lady Williams told us. And I have not the foggiest idea how she knew. You will have to ask her."

"I will. But it makes no sense. He was Lady Carrington's paramour. Why would he want to kill her?"

"Because he was not her only one."

Chapter Eleven

Sketches by Aubrey Beardsley

We departed the Langham and stood in the shade offered by its arched portico adjacent to Portland Place. Holmes queried me and the inspector.

"Inspector," he said, "I could not help but notice that you were watching Madame closely and said nothing. Any insights, sir?"

He shook his head. "For the past twenty years, I have dealt only with soldiers. I worked in military policing and intelligence. Soldiers are clumsy liars, and spies know they cannot put lies in their reports as that is the way that soldiers end up dead. I have a lot to learn about civilians who kill those they are not at war with, and I do not know what to make of that woman."

"And you, Watson?"

"I felt that she was telling us the truth about pouring herself a glass of Port just before leaving. That would put her off the list of those who might have poisoned the bottle."

"No, my dear Watson," said Holmes. "It only means that she may have been the first to have had the opportunity of doing so, after having taken the last untainted glass."

"Oh, yes, well, I suppose you're right. Well, then, what I did not understand was her trying to implicate Dr. Sterndale. He would have had to have entered the room unseen as everyone was leaving, put poison in the bottle, and escape before Lady Carrington and Mildred sat down. That seems too far-fetched."

Holmes lit a cigarette and said nothing for a minute.

"An excellent point, Watson. Likely true, but let us not forget that a man who can stalk a lion in the jungle without even letting his scent be noticed should have no trouble slipping in and out of a house. Perhaps we should add him to our list. Speaking of which, the next name will be expecting us after lunch."

Saxon Sydenham's address was also in Bermondsey, two blocks to the east of Lady Carrington's along the side of the Thames. I thought that odd, as he was known to be an impresario who had successfully and profitably managed many popular musical and theatrical events. His wealth put him somewhat out-of-place in a working-class neighborhood. That puzzle was answered when we arrived at his front door. The houses on either side of it had small notices on their doors, accompanied by arrows, informing the visitor that the central door was the one on which to knock.

"Does he need three houses?" I asked.

"It would appear that he bought all three," said Holmes, "and remodeled them into one very spacious home. He has a reputation for cultivated and expensive taste and sent a note back to me saying how deeply thrilled he would be to entertain us."

Holmes knocked on the door, and we were welcomed by a maid who could not have been out of her teen years. All three of us were caught speechless for a second by her scandalous costume. It was a maid's uniform, black and trimmed with white lace, alarmingly low-cut in the bodice and high-cut in the flared skirt. She was utterly unselfconscious and offered a coquettish smile.

"*Bonjour,*" she chirped. "*Entrez, messieurs. Suivez-moi, s'il vous plaît.*"

We followed her into the creatively-appointed parlor, where she gestured to the chairs.

"*Un peu de cognac pour vous détendre, messieurs?*"

"Thank you," said Holmes. "However, we are here to speak with Mr. Sydenham. Will you kindly let him know that we are waiting for him?"

"*Un instant s'il vous plaît. Je ferai savoir à mon maître,*" she, smiled and vanished up the stairs.

We waited for another five minutes, and I glanced around the room and noted the original paintings filling every empty space on the walls. I recognized a few of them as having been painted by the members of the Pre-Raphaelite Brotherhood, along with a few sketches by Aubrey Beardsley that were of questionable taste. Books and magazines were carefully laid out on the coffee table and end tables, and a number of busts and small statues were tucked into every nook and corner.

"This man," I whispered to Holmes, "has excellent taste."

"It can be bought."

I was about to chide Holmes for his cynicism, but a gentleman entered the room. Although the noon hour was approaching, he was clad in a royal-blue silk-brocade dressing gown that had oriental designs woven into it in gold, red, and yellow. His feet were shod only with sandals, leaving his ankles and lower calves bare and exposed.

The man himself was remarkably handsome, clean-shaven, with an athletic frame and dashes of white hair gracing his temples. He was a tall as Holmes, but much broader in the shoulders and appeared to have reached a mature station in life without having acquired the almost ubiquitous pot-belly that was the hallmark of middle-aged Englishmen of means.

In his one hand, he held a lit cigar and in his other a tumbler, partly filled with an amber liquid that I guessed was a single malt Scotch. The scent of a select men's cologne—*4711* was the brand, I thought—mixed with the aroma of the cigar to create a not unpleasant odor.

"Good morning, gentleman," he said in a rich bass voice. "Saxon Sydenham at your service. Welcome to my humble abode. I am honored by a visit of such esteemed men. Please, make yourselves comfortable. Did Mimi offer you some Cognac?"

He turned and called in the direction of the kitchen. "*Mimi, ma petite.*"

"*Je viens, maître.*"

The young maid reappeared bearing a silver tray on which were three full snifters of Cognac and one glass tumbler filled, I assumed with more Scotch. She approached us, and rather than bending over and exposing a shocking degree of cleavage, with perfect balance and poise, she dropped to her knees in front of the three of use and extended the tray in our direction. We each took a snifter, and then she gracefully returned to her feet, stepped over to Mr. Sydenham, who by now was ensconced in a large arm-chair, took his nearly empty glass and handed him the full one.

"*Merci, mon petit choux,*" he said and lightly caressed her cheek.

"Now then, gentlemen," he said, smiling at us with a remarkably white set of perfectly aligned teeth. "How may I be of service to you?"

"We have," said Holmes, "a few questions regarding the event at Lady Carrington's that took place on Saturday evening. I believe that you were present."

"And I believe," he said, after a sip of his Scotch, "that Sherlock Holmes would not be paying me a visit if I were not there. Please, sir. Ask away. The floor is yours."

"My colleague, Inspector Farber of Scotland Yard," said Holmes, nodding toward the inspector, "has some preliminary questions."

Before the inspector could start, our host queried him.

"Your name is Farber?"

"It is."

"I thought I had met all of the current inspectors at Scotland Yard, but I do not recall having the privilege of your acquaintance, sir."

"I am on secondment from Her Majesty's Military Police."

"Oh, why that's splendid. I have always had a deep admiration for the men who serve in our military forces. My father rose to the rank of a colonel under the Raj. I tried to follow in his footsteps, but I fear my time of service was all too short."

"What regiment," I said, "if I may ask?"

He laughed and took another sip. "My time was exceptionally brief. I never made it past cadet, and then I was unceremoniously expelled." He laughed and was obviously intent on recounting his adventure.

"Ah, yes. I was a cadet at the barracks in Karachi. What a rum bunch of lads we were. But in the armory in which we trained, a motto had been painted across the top of the wall. It read, *Dulce et decorum est pro patria mori*. I confess, I thought it was the stupidest thing I had ever heard. So, one night, several of us—and I confess, I was the ringleader—got a ladder and some paint and changed it to read *Dulce et decorum est bastardus ut alterum pro patria mori*. It is sweet and fitting to make the other bastard die for his country."

Having said this, he laughed heartily. "The sergeant in charge of the cadets concluded that I was not and never would be fit to be an officer and had me turfed out. I cannot begin to express my gratitude to him." He laughed again.

"Shall we," said the inspector, "leave your military career behind and return to the evening of the ninth of June."

"As you wish. Why not? Yes, I was there throughout. It was simply a marvelous party. Dear Gwendolyn does know how to lay out a wonderful spread. Quite the witty, cultivated crowd of progressive, enlightened artists. I couldn't have liked it more."

"Did you," asked Inspector Farber, "regularly attend such events at Lady Carrington's?"

"No, my dear fellow, I did not. It was my first opportunity, and I had a smashing good time."

"Why were you there?"

"Because I was invited."

"I shall pose my question again, sir, and I request that you not be so flippant. You had no connection to the *Review,* so why were you present."

"*Au contraire, mon ami.* I have a very strong connection to the *Cornwall Monthly Review.* I own it."

We stared at him. He smiled smugly and raised his glass in a toast toward us.

"What do you mean by that?" said Holmes. "Lady Carrington was the sole owner."

"Right you are, Mr. Holmes. She *was.* A week ago, she sold it to me. Lock, stock and barrel as they say in America."

"Do you have documents—"

"Such as a copy of the *Agreement of Sale and Purchase*, Mr. Holmes? By sheer coincidence, I do. And as I expected your disbelief, I put it in a file, which you will find on the end table beside you. Please, look it over. You too, Doctor. Perhaps you would like to submit a story to me about the misadventures of Sherlock Holmes."

He laughed, somewhat more loudly than was necessary, raised his glass again and then took a gulp.

Holmes opened the file and read the contents, passing each page over to me when he had finished with it, and I, in turn, passed it along to Inspector Farber. There was no question. Lady Carrington had signed the Agreement a week ago, accepting payment of one hundred thousand pounds for all current assets of her journal.

"I am sure, sir," said Holmes, "you will appreciate that in light of Lady Carrington's murder, this transaction is material to the case we are investigating."

"Which is why I had it ready and waiting for your brilliant investigative mind to examine."

"Why," said Holmes, "did you buy it? That is an exorbitant price to pay for a literary journal."

"Not, Mr. Holmes, not if what you purchase is the pearl of great price. My entire life has been spent promoting the arts and culture of our sceptered isle. The *Cornwall Review* has become a treasured gem that is truly loved by so many thousands of British men and women who believe passionately in the beauty of the English language and the brilliance of the imagination of our best writers. Lady Gwendolyn was about to abandon it and let it fade into obscurity as she sailed off to Africa with He-Who-Must-Be-Obeyed. I could not let that happen. Even though I may never recover my investment, I did my duty. I did it for my country and my culture. So, no price was too high."

"How wonderfully patriotic of you."

"Thank you, sir. Perhaps you can persuade your dear friend, Dr. Watson, to consider sending one of his excellent stories our way. We could match the rates offered by the *Strand,* and we could guarantee that he would reach tens of thousands of new readers who have yet to hear of the heroic triumphs of Sherlock Holmes."

"I am sure he will give your offer thoughtful consideration. However, there is one item in your Agreement with Lady Carrington that puzzles me."

"And what might that be, sir?"

"This contract was signed over a week ago. Why have you not acted on it yet? All assets of the *Review* remain in Lady Carrington's home. Why have you not taken control of them?"

"Read the fine print, Mr. Holmes. The seller has ten days from the signing of the contract to hand over everything—the contracts with the writers and staff, the subscription lists, the agreements with newsagents, the contents of future issues that are already edited and ready for publication, and the contracts with advertisers. As of Monday morning, I shall pay a collection call and remove all the assets. As of Tuesday, I shall be the editor and publisher. Any further questions, sir?"

"Yes. One more. Is there any reason why you should not be considered a suspect in the murder of Lady Carrington?"

Mr. Saxon Sydenham laughed jovially. "Oh my, but you detective chaps have such nasty, suspicious minds. I suppose that is a necessary trait of your profession. So, yes. Add me to your list. Clearly, being one of the last to leave the party, I had the opportunity. But my relationship with Her Ladyship was only one of amiable business people conducting mutually beneficial transactions in good faith. Wherein is my motive to kill her? And furthermore, let me suggest that you investigate every contract I have engaged in during the past decade. You will find that I have never lifted a finger to strike anyone, friend or foe. That is why God made lawyers."

He laughed once again and drained his glass.

Chapter Twelve

The Return of the Review

The three of us found a nearby pub in which to have a pint and chat.

"Quite the decent thing to do," I said. "I can't tell how he made his fortune, but he seems genuinely committed to the promotion of the arts."

"I can't say," added Inspector Farber, "that I like the chap. A bit too much on the lazy and self-indulgent side, if you ask me. He wouldn't last a day in my regiment. But his act strikes me as being high-minded and patriotic."

Holmes sighed loudly. "Good heavens. What is wrong with the two of you? Cannot you see that the *Review* is a gold mine? It is luscious low-hanging fruit, ripe for the picking. Choose your metaphor. It is worth many times more than what he paid for it, and dear Lady Carrington was too simple-minded to know better. All she wanted was to get a boat-load of cash so she could run off to Africa."

"But … but," I said, "it has only been this past year that each issue has become profitable. What are you talking about?"

The inspector grunted his agreement with me.

"Ah, I see that the two of you are not students of the business of arts and culture. Allow me to teach you a lesson. It appears that brilliant Miss Smith has built the journal into the one with the highest subscription in all of England. It now surpasses the *Strand*. Seven hundred and fifty thousand people pay for a copy every month. But not much, you say. Only two shillings a month with a discount to one pound if they pay an entire year in advance. That, gentlemen, adds up to three-quarters of a million pounds. Do they sell advertisements?"

"They all do now," I said. "The S*trand* began two years ago. Everything from chocolates to corsets can be found between the pages of my stories."

"And the income from them," said Holmes, "runs about equal with what is received from subscriptions. That adds up to one million and a half pounds every year for her *Review*. Furthermore, Miss Smith, so you tell me, Watson, has built an inventory of essays, poems, stories, serial biographies and nasty satires enough to last an entire year. So, starting the minute he owns the *Review*, he will terminate all the writers, have some young servant—even his *petite Mimi* could do it—assemble a mixture of a dozen articles per issue, pay only for printing and the post, and put a million pounds in his pocket."

I gasped. "That's a fortune for doing next to nothing."

"It is, and I am not finished. At the end of the year, he will run a campaign to renew the subscriptions, and the readers and advertisers will all sign up again. That is another million and a half pounds. Are you following me? Then he hires a group of hack writers, pays them a few shillings and sends out another dozen issues. The quality is terrible, but he will still make an enormous profit."

"But the readership will be destroyed. The business will have lost its value," I said.

"So what? He will sell the list to any other publisher—the *Strand* would be thrilled to own it—for two hundred thousand pounds, and he will have made a fortune and done almost no work whatsoever."

The three of us sat and pondered what we had just heard.

Holmes carried on. "It is possible that with Lady Carrington's death, both her solicitor and Clapper's might be able to make a case before a magistrate that it was her intent, after receiving legal counsel, not to agree to the contract. It would be my guess, however, that the law would be more on the side of our impresario than her step-brother."

"What if he forged it?"

Holmes paused and took a sip of his ale. "An excellent question. Does he strike you as the type of man who would be so unscrupulous as to take advantage of a woman's tragic death to forge a document and, by doing so, enrich himself and impoverish her estate?"

Farber and I looked at each other, and both of us nodded.

"I agree," said Holmes. "It is a possibility. If he did, the contract would be null and void, but I cannot think of any way we could prove a forged document before it's execution on Monday. Any suggestions, Inspector Farber?"

"I assume," said Farber, "that you would compare her signature with documents that were unquestionably signed by her. Who was her personal solicitor?"

"I do not know, but I am reasonably certain that our two ladies would. Watson, would you be so kind as to contact them this evening and ask if they could meet us again tomorrow morning?"

"Happy to. May I suggest the Savoy?"

"Brilliant."

Chapter Thirteen

They're All in Cornwall

I arranged the meeting Holmes had requested for nine o'clock but asked Mildred Smith if she could meet me an hour earlier. She had already been distressed by the murder of Lady Carrington and the news about Thoby MacCarthy. I wanted to warn her in advance of the sale of her beloved *Review* to Saxon Sydenham.

As I had feared, she was very upset by that news. I tried to soften the blow by suggesting that Holmes was going to investigate the possibility of a forgery. My efforts were to no avail. She clenched her fists, and her body tightened. Tears seeped out of her eyes, and she dabbed her eyes with her serviette. Then she looked at me and shook her head.

"No. I cannot believe she would do that. It is not possible," she said.

"Are you saying that you believe it is a forged contract?"

"It must be. Granted, Gwendolyn was distracted of late. All she could think about was an exciting new life, waited on hand and foot by Ubangis in Africa with her great white hunter. She had a meeting with that Saxon fellow the previous week, but I cannot believe that she had agreed to sell our *Review* and say nothing to me about it. How much did he claim he paid for it?"

I told her the figure we had seen in the contract.

She shook her head. "I find it hard to believe that Gwendolyn was so naïve that she would sell for much less than it is worth. The right to use the name alone is worth that much."

"The contract also," I said, "included all the assets." I listed them off as I had seen them in the document.

"Does Mr. Holmes think it could be a forgery? Pray God, he is right."

"Let us hope," I said, "that he will turn up evidence that will annul the sale. And if not, and if you cannot work for Clive Clapper, you could just start your own periodical. You have all the knowledge and expertise and connections. You could do it. I'm sure you could."

"Oh, John. Thank you. But it takes far more than that. It takes capital. The *Cornwall Monthly Review* lost money for over fifteen years. Gwendolyn covered the losses, and we built the subscriptions and advertising income slowly. I am in no position to do that on my own."

Against my better judgment, I offered to ride to her rescue.

"I am not exactly a poor man these days. I could help you."

She sighed, let her shoulders sag, and then looked up at me and smiled. "My dear John, I'm sorry. Right now, I am terribly vulnerable, and my mother warned me against letting myself become financially and emotionally dependent on a man when feeling utterly weak. It is too easy to believe you are falling in love, when all you are doing is falling into servitude. Such liaisons never end well."

"I can think," I said, "of worse things than—"

I did not get to finish my statement as Holmes and Farber appeared in the entrance of the hotel. They were accompanied by Mrs. Sheridan and came directly to the table where Millie and I were sitting.

After a brief chat over coffee and the Savoy's famous French pastries, Holmes moved directly to the purpose of the meeting. He informed the two women of the sale of the *Review* to Sydenham and his suspicions that the contract could have been forged.

"What we need," he said, "is access to as many other documents signed by Lady Carrington as we can find so we can make a conclusive comparison of the signatures. Mrs. Sheridan, as the manager of her household and personal affairs, I assume you know where some such documents can be found. Miss Smith, as the editor of the publication, you must have agreements with writers, printers, advertisers and all the rest on file and signed by Her Ladyship. Could you kindly take us to those documents straight away so that this matter can be put to rest one way or the other?"

I had expected that both of them would respond at once and offer to take us back to the house in Bermondsey and to the appropriate files. They did not. Instead, they looked somewhat ill at ease and then looked at each other. Mrs. Sheridan replied first.

"Inasmuch as we would both wish to help—and I am sure I speak for Miss Smith as well as myself—there are some difficulties in agreeing to your request."

"Madam," said Holmes, "again, I appreciate and admire your desire to maintain your pledge of confidentiality to Lady Carrington. However, my request is only for the purpose of making sure that her wishes are followed. There is no harm that can come to her reputation by helping me."

"That is not it at all, Mr. Holmes," said Mrs. Sheridan. "We would—and again, I am sure I speak for both of us—be more than happy to help, but we may not be of much use to you."

"And why not?"

"I cannot think of a single document in the house that bears her handwriting or signature. Every agreement with the landlord, or staff of the house, or contractors making repairs that was made during the past seven years was signed by me as her legally appointed agent. Any personal notes she sent, she typed, including her name. Records that were more than seven years old were routinely destroyed. She valued her privacy highly and did not want any future busybody from the press snooping into the private affairs of her earlier life."

"It was the same for me, sir," said Miss Smith. "I handled all of the negotiations and agreements with printers, subscribers, advertisers, bookstore, newsagents and the like, and all of our writers. I have been doing so for nearly twenty years. There is not a single document connected to our *Review* that bears her signature."

"Good heavens," said Holmes, "there must be something. What about her property deeds, her assigning power of attorney, her Last Will and Testament? She must have signed those in person, and they must still be on file somewhere."

"If they exist," said Mrs. Sheridan. "they will be kept at her estate in Cornwall and with the family solicitor in Penzance. You will have to go there if you wish to examine them."

Holmes said nothing for a minute as he sat motionless and closed his eyes. He nodded his head ever so slightly and opened his eyes.

"Proving whether the sale was forged or legitimate either makes Mr. Sydenham my primary suspect or removes him from the list. If paying a visit to Cornwall is the only way that can be established, it is imperative that we do so. You two ladies are familiar with Lady Carrington's private affairs. We are not. Might I impose on the two of you to come to Cornwall with us?"

"I regret, Mr. Holmes, that I cannot oblige," said Mrs. Sheridan. "I have never been to Her Ladyship's estate there and would be of no use and, furthermore, I have accepted a new position helping to manage the household of Baron and Lady Creston. My first day in that situation is Monday. I fear I cannot be in Penzance when I should be in Mayfair."

"I can go," said Mildred Smith. "I have not been down there this year, but I lived on her estate for several years, and I know her solicitor. When do you want to leave?"

"We have two more interviews scheduled for today," said Holmes. "Could you be ready to go first thing tomorrow morning?"

"If that is what you wish, Mr. Holmes. If my memory serves me correctly, the first train leaves from Paddington at seven. Shall I meet you there?"

"Thank you," said Holmes. "Your assistance is appreciated."

The two women departed the Savoy and Holmes, Farber and I had another cup of coffee and finished off the basket of pastries.

"Do you wish," said Holmes to Farber, "to accompany us to Cornwall?"

"I will come with you today to the interviews with Lady Williams and Rev. Chrisparkle, but, if you don't mind, I shall pass on the excursion to Cornwall. There is nothing I could add to your investigation there, and I believe my time would be better spent acquiring as much data as possible on both Mr. Clapper and Mr. Sydenham. So far, they are the two who believed themselves to be the beneficiaries of Lady Carrington's death, and therefore they remain at the top of my list, Mr. Holmes."

"I agree wholeheartedly," said Holmes. "Very well then, we have an appointment in half-an-hour with Lady Williams."

Chapter Fourteen

We Had the Same Tutor

From the Savoy, we walked north past the shops of Southampton Street and into Covent Garden. A pretty young woman with a painful Cockney accent attempted to sell us flowers, but we declined and continued on past the British Museum and into Fitzrovia.

Lady Mary Williams's house was on a small street just off of Charlotte and north of Goodge Street. It was a whitewashed terraced house, somewhat above average in size and of the style that lesser members of the nobility owned or rented whilst living in London and not on their estates in the country.

The maid who greeted us at the door might be charitably described as no-longer-young and no-longer-small but cheerful all the same.

"Do come in now," she said in a thick Scottish accent. "Her Ladyship's been expecting you. Here now, just follow me to the parlor and sit down, and I'll organize a wee spot of tea and some shortbread for you."

The furniture in the room struck me as possibly having been purchased the week before from the shops boasting the latest, sleek and stylish fashion, except for the chairs that were covered in what I thought was the Mackenzie tartan. The wood trim was thin and the lines plain and, as confirmed by my backside, miserably uncomfortable to be sat on for more than five minutes.

We waited ten minutes for Lady Williams to make her entry.

She was an attractive woman with a slender figure that was accentuated by a waistline constricted by what must have been an exceptionally uncomfortable corset, providing her with what the American wags had described as 'looking like a wasp.' Her luxurious chestnut hair was bunched on top of her head such that it ballooned out over her skull like a small inner tube wrapped in filament. She had a cigarette holder in her one hand, with a smoldering cigarette attached, and a fan in her other. I thought that she might have been described as being the epitome of elegant 'Gibson Girl' fashion if it were not for the fact that she struck me as a woman who was doing a commendable job of holding on to her disappearing youth.

We stood to greet her.

"Ah yes," she said, "what have we here? The famous duo of Mr. Sherlock Holmes and Dr. Watson and another man who appears sufficiently disheveled to be a police inspector. Such a pleasant diversion on an otherwise boring morning. What is it you men want to know about the utterly horrid death of my dear old friend, Gwendolyn? Oh, and do sit down."

Her faint accent was not from Cornwall and more like Edinburgh.

She partially sat and partially reclined on a day bed and tucked her legs up on the cushion beside her.

"We can start, Lady Williams," said Inspector Farber, "by your telling us what your relationship was with Lady Carrington and why you were at her home on Saturday evening."

"Oh, can we now? Very well, then." She took a slow draft on her cigarette, adjusted her position on the couch and responded. "Gwendolyn and I have known each other since our childhood in

Cornwall. Her family owned one vast estate there, and mine owned the smaller one beside it. Being girls of the same age and the only two from titled families, we were thrown together by our governesses. She had no siblings. I had six but they were all younger and my cousins had all decamped and moved to Nova Scotia. Having no other friends, as we were tutored and did not attend school, we had no choice but to spend our days together and thus became friends. What else do you want to know?"

"About your being at her home last weekend. Were you—"

"Oh, yes, that. Well, as girls we had the same tutor, dear Miss Hazel, who drilled us on grammar and penmanship and syntax and nouns and verbs and participles and much more. Well, she somehow put it into our heads that we had a future as women writers. There has been a goodly number over the last few decades, you know. So, after having acquired sufficiently interesting and adequately wealthy husbands for ourselves, we set out to conquer the battlefield—almost entirely populated by men—of authoring and publishing. My interest ran more to investigating the biographies of fascinating women and hers to building the *Review*. I wrote chapters she and our readers found somewhat salacious and thus irresistible, and she published them. I was one of her dependable contributors and thus always invited to her *soirées*. I'm sorry if I cannot come up with a more intriguing reason for my being there. But if you ask me tomorrow, I can likely offer you a better one."

"That will do, Madam," said Farber.

"If I may," said Holmes before the inspector could pose his next question, "permit me to ask you if it was Lady Carrington who approved of and chose to publish your chapters, or was it Miss Smith?"

She inhaled and long, languorous draft on her cigarette and slowly blew it out in a stream toward the ceiling. "If you are half as smart a detective, Mr. Holmes, as your friend's stories about you in the *Strand* make you out to be, you already know that Mildred Smith was the genius behind the *Review*."

"And she approved your somewhat racy account of the life of Lucrezia Borgia?"

"She loved it. Truth be told, she made my chapters far more polished and more titillating than I had written them, to my eternal gratitude as I have become a much sought-after guest at no end of *soirées* hosted by the self-aggrandized and fashionably decadent crowd."

"Aren't you fortunate," said Holmes. "You will, I trust, permit me to ask a question concerning a matter in which neither you nor Lady Carrington appear to have been particularly lucky. Both of you are married women, but neither of you appear to have a husband present in your lives. Why not?"

Another long draft on her cigarette preceded her answer.

"When Gwendolyn was twenty, she married the splendidly rich and boring Lord Chester Carrington. They got along famously until fifteen years ago when he decided that he no longer found it amusing to have an emancipated progressive wife and demanded that she give up her journal, start bearing offspring, and act like a normal wife of the landed gentry."

"I cannot imagine," said Holmes, "that she was pleased with that."

"That, Mr. Holmes, would be an understatement. For a year, they fought like cats and dogs, and then, thank the gods and goddesses, he had a violent seizure one night after dinner and promptly died, leaving her wonderfully wealthy, free as a bird, and happy as a lark."

"And you? Where is your husband?"

"Oh, well, I thought you were going to say 'For thou hast had five husbands; and he whom thou now hast is not thy husband.' Pity, I only ever had one. He and I choose to live apart and maintain separate lives. He looks after the family properties, and I enjoy life in the city. It is not an uncommon arrangement amongst wives and husbands of our class and persuasion, Mr. Holmes."

"Why have you not sought a divorce?"

"On come now, Mr. Holmes. To be estranged from one's spouse is commonplace. To be divorced is to lose one's status, respect, and social rank. Who would want to do that?"

"If you say so. Now then, when did you depart from the house?"

"Not long after nine. Perhaps twenty-five- or thirty-minutes past."

"Why did you leave early?"

"I had become bored. The interesting people were all leaving, and I feared that I would be subjected to another reading by Little Miss Clapper. I am fond of the girl, but her poetry is god-awful."

"Lady Carrington was poisoned sometime later that evening. Can you suggest, in confidence, whom you suspect might have wanted her dead and for what reason?"

Another long stream of cigarette smoke, and she answered. "Clive, of course. He stood to inherit all the wealth along with the *Review*. And, well, if he is at the top of my list, we cannot exclude his precocious daughter, can we?"

"Madam," said Inspector Farber, "kindly refrain from being flippant. This is a murder investigation."

"Who says I am being flippant? That clever child already had a score of her murder mysteries published. She imagined more diabolical ways to kill characters off than I ever knew existed and is quite the little expert on all forms of poison. And what child would not want her father to become fabulously rich?"

"Miss Smith," said Holmes, "almost died as well."

"Oh, yes, well then, right you are. Knock Felicity off the list. She worshipped Mildred like a pathetic puppy dog."

"Any other suggestions?"

"None at the moment. But ask me tomorrow, and I may have one by then."

"Are you aware than Lady Carrington had sold the *Review* and all its assets to Mr. Saxon Sydenham during the week before the *soirée*?"

She raised her cigarette holder to her lips but held it an inch away and, for a moment, did not reply.

"No, I did not. Are you sure of that?"

"He has a signed contract, and he says they agreed on the terms."

"Well, he would say that, wouldn't he?"

Holmes concluded the interview, and we rose and departed the parlor. Lady Williams did not get up from her day bed to see us out.

We were about to leave through the front door when Holmes stopped and stood still. He appeared to have fixed his gaze on the glass side-panel to the left of the door. Then he turned around and shouted up the stairs.

"DOCTOR STERNDALE! Kindly come down and say hello."

Chapter Fifteen

Bwana Sterndale

I was speechless and was about to say something when Lady Williams, having heard Holmes bellowing, came and joined us by the front door. Now she turned and faced the staircase and shouted.

"Leon! You may as well come down. He's Sherlock Holmes, and he knows you're here!"

At the top of the stairs, the tall, thick figure of Dr. Leon Sterndale emerged and began to descend. He was glaring at Holmes.

"How did you know I was here?"

"That is what you must expect when——"

"Leon, for pity sake," said Lady Williams, "how stupid can you be? I told you not to leave your stick in the umbrella stand."

My head turned immediately toward the left side of the door, and there, mixed in with a half-dozen umbrellas, was a gnarled ebony walking stick.

Sterndale stepped off the final stair and approached Holmes.

"Hello, Holmes. Now you know where I live and to whom I am married. What else do you want to know?"

"Perhaps you could begin by explaining to me how it is that you were formerly living in the home of your paramour and after her death moved back into the home of your wife, who just happens to have been the lifelong dearest friend of Lady Carrington?"

"None of your bloody business."

"Well then," said Lady Williams, using her cigarette holder like a schoolmarm's pointer, "I can."

She took yet another slow draft and this time exhaled the smoke in a series of smoke rings.

"It all began some twenty-five years ago. Leon was a handsome, virile and penniless country doctor, and I was a naïve twenty-year-old maiden who was swept off my feet, and I married him. After two years of what I thought was marital bliss, he became besotted with one of the local farm girls—a beauty mind you—named Brenda Tregennis."

"That's enough!" said Sterndale. "There is no need—"

"Oh, but there is, dear husband. Mr. Holmes and Scotland Yard are conducting a murder investigation, and all the sordid secrets have to be exposed. My husband's fervent lover then went and had herself asphyxiated by her brother, and poor Leon was all alone again. Instead of trying to re-establish a marriage, he then became besotted with Gwendolyn, and now she's dead. Poor boy."

"Enough, Mary!" Sterndale cried. "For God's sake, keep your tongue in your head."

Holmes was looking back and forth between the two of them and seeming somewhat confused.

"Would one of you explain to me how it is that the three of you co-existed sharing homes and wives and a husband and continuing to work together?"

"I was fully content," said Lady Williams, "to let Gwendolyn amuse herself with Leon. She tires quickly of her toys. And he does have some assets that she found satisfying."

"For god's sake woman!" Sterndale started to walk toward Lady Williams, his fists clenched. Holmes stepped in between them. I was afraid that blows were about to be exchanged, and I would not have placed a penny on Holmes's coming out the victor, but Lady Williams laughed and stood directly in front of her husband.

"It is quite all right, gentlemen," she said. "Leon knows what side his bread is buttered on. Our properties are held in a trust established by my father, who was wise enough to see what type of a man I had married."

With an effort, Sterndale mastered himself and spoke.

"Now you see, Mr. Holmes, what I could not fully explain three years ago when we met in Cornwall. I can never again love my wife, and I can never hope to regain the passionate love I had for Brenda Tregennis, and by the deplorable laws of England, I cannot obtain a divorce. However, I assure you, I cared deeply for Gwendolyn Carrington, regardless of what my wife says about her. My only wish is that you hurry and find who killed her. And if you don't, I will."

Chapter Sixteen

The View from the Pew

Our time in Lady Williams's house had taken longer than Holmes had expected, and once outside, we hailed a cab to return to Bermondsey. As we hurried south back across the Thames, Inspector Farber turned to Holmes and me.

"Who are these people? They have the morals of an alley cat."

"Welcome, my dear Inspector," said Holmes, "to the progressive, liberated, emancipated artistic aesthetes of London. They are highly self-absorbed and pride themselves in being unconstrained by conventional behavior."

"And this Sterndale fellow? You have dealt with him before, I gather."

"We have, and during that adventure, the good doctor and I almost died."

"That is such a comforting piece of data, Mr. Holmes. Is there anything else I should know before we meet the next suspect?"

"Only that of all those who were present at the *soirée*, he is the one I am reasonably certain is not a suspect."

"Then why are we meeting with him?"

"Like all convivial men of the cloth, he is likely to be a font of information."

We bumped along over the Tower Bridge and on into Bermondsey. We were approaching Jamaica Street when Holmes turned to me.

"What do you know about Lucrezia Borgia?" he asked me.

"Not much. Daughter of the Pope. One of the most beautiful women of the Renaissance. Had a slew of husbands and lovers. Why?"

"Several of those men died. It is said that she poisoned them."

The St. James Church in Bermondsey looked more like a Greek temple than an Anglican church and bore the strange ornament of a large, gilded dragon at the top of its steeple. It sat in the center of an oasis of green grass and trees in the midst of a crowded, poor neighborhood. We ascended the steps and opened the massive doors to the sanctuary.

"Was Rev. Chrisparkle," I asked, "not available to meet us in his office? It would have been much more private."

"His note," said Holmes, "told me that he would be pleased to meet but that he was terribly busy. It appears that he is preparing for two funerals tomorrow."

"Oh dear, I hope it was only a couple of his elderly parishioners and nothing too tragic."

"My dear Watson, please," said Holmes.

I looked at him and could see a look of benign condescension coming my way.

"What?" I said, and then a light flashed in my brain. "Oh, yes, of course, there have been two of them—Carrington and MacCarthy.

Both from his parish. Right. I don't suppose you are planning to attend the services, are you?"

"Oh, Watson, please."

"What this time? Oh…yes…we are off to Cornwall tomorrow, aren't we?"

"Yes, Watson."

The interior of the church, though not large, had stunning height and was remarkably light, with sunlight streaming in from the clerestory windows. Above the altar, on the wall of the apse, was a magnificent portrait of Our Lord as he ascended into heaven. With the exception of two people moving around up by the altar, the sanctuary was empty.

"Reverend Chrisparkle!" said Holmes, his voice echoing in the empty nave.

A man beside the altar, dressed in a simple black shirt and trousers, looked up, as did the woman who was polishing the altar rail.

"Is that Mr. Holmes?" the chap called back in a deep, resonant voice. "Come on up. We can chat whilst we work."

The three of us walked up the center aisle. The familiar musty odor of an old church was overtaken by the mix of lemon oil and brass polish.

"Dreadfully sorry," said the vicar, "That we cannot stop for tea, but if you will sit in the first pew, we can talk whilst Margaret and I get ready for tomorrow."

We sat in the row closest to the altar rail as he sorted out a stack of the Book of Common Prayer, and a woman, who I guessed was his wife, polished the brass and woodwork.

"We regret having to disturb you," said Holmes. "We understand that you are under some pressure, and we appreciate your agreeing to meet with us."

"Happy to see you," came the response from the altar platform. "Normally, when I preach a sermon, that pew is always empty. Nice for a change to see three chaps sitting in it. Oh, this is my wife,

Margaret. Margaret, the thin fellow is Mr. Sherlock Holmes, and the portly one is Dr. Watson. And, I do apologize, sir, but I do not know who you are."

"Inspector Farber, Scotland Yard," said the third member of our trio.

The vicar was a large man, somewhat roundish and somewhat reddish, the sort of fifty-year-old jovial-looking minister that one tended to imagine would serve out his life in a country parish tending to the needs of his parishioners. His wife was a plain-looking woman also dressed in black, with a head of silver hair and gold-rimmed glasses perched on her nose. She smiled warmly at us but said nothing.

"As your time, sir, is already spoken for," said Holmes in a voice loud enough to carry from the pew to the apse, "please forgive me if we skip any preliminary questions and go straight to the heart of the matter."

"Let me guess," said Chrisparkle with a friendly chuckle. "you want to know what a man of the cloth was doing in such an unholy gathering and consorting with such reprobate people."

"I might not have phrased it that way," said Holmes, "but that would be an excellent place to start."

"And surely, I have been criticized and murmured against for associating with that crowd, but I have the example of Our Lord who faced the same for associating with publicans and sinners and tax-collectors. He told his critics that he had come not to call the righteous but sinners to repentance. So, I think I have good grounds for trying to do the same." He continued to insert small flyers into the stack of prayer books as he spoke.

"From everything I've learned about them," said Inspector Farber, "they are a rather depraved cast of characters."

"And," said the vicar, "let him who is without sin amongst us stone the first cast." When he said this, he gave the three of us a friendly but steady looking-over as if to remind us that none of us were without our moral failings.

"Indeed," said Holmes, "we are all members of a fallen race. But last Saturday evening, one member of that cast fell more than the rest of them and committed murder. Forgive me, sir, if I am not interested in your theological insights. What I want to know is who you consider most likely to have killed Lady Carrington."

The reverend looked straight back at Holmes and slowly put the prayer book he had in his hands on the pile. He approached the altar rail, and in a surprisingly nimble move for a man his size and age, he sat down on the floor of the altar platform, stuck his feet under the rail, and planted them on the kneeling pad. Then he rested his forearms of the altar rail and leaned forward. He was about to say something when his wife let out an exasperated sigh.

"Edward," she said, "I just wiped that down."

"Not to worry, Margaret, darling. I shall make sure it is spotless. Now then, Mr. Holmes, that is a hard question, and one that I admit has preoccupied my thinking even when I should have been devoting my time to prayer and sermon preparation."

"I am all attention," said Holmes. "Kindly enlighten us as to your conclusions."

Chapter Seventeen

The Vicar's Wife Suspects

"Well, it's complicated, sir. I remember reading somewhere when I was a boy about some chap who told his assistant that when you eliminate the impossible, whatever remains, however improbable, must be the truth."

In my mind, I was smirking. Holmes was not smiling.

"An excellent principle," he said. "Please carry on and tell us what you concluded."

"Very well, then, I shall begin with myself. I know I did not murder anyone, and even if I had wanted to, I left well before the deed was done, as did Lady Williams. So, the two of us are out.

"So is Thoby MacCarthy. He had been to see me several times since the year began. He knew he was not long for this world and would soon be passing into eternity. I cannot believe that he would want to stand before Almighty God, having just murdered someone. It does tend to reduce one's prospects for getting your white robe and mansion. The funeral I am going to conduct for him tomorrow is pretty well according to his plan."

"He planned his own funeral?" I said.

"Yes, he did, and true to form, he dictated what words I was to say in my opening welcome. I am to say, and I quote. 'Mr. Thoby MacCarthy has told me to welcome you and thank you for coming to his funeral, and he wants you to know that for damn sure he is not coming to yours.'"

The three of us laughed, and the vicar carried on.

"Spot on, I'd say. Now there is something you should know about Lady Williams."

"Edward!" His wife was scowling.

"It is all right, darling. I'm not violating any penitent privilege, only passing along gossip."

Her scowl did not fade. He continued.

"What do you know about a chap named Dr. Sterndale?"

"I am well-acquainted with him," said Holmes.

"Ah, so you have met Leon-the-lion-hunter. Spot on. You know that he is married to Lady Williams?"

"I do."

"And you know that the mistress he used to keep in Cornwall died three years ago?"

"I do," said Holmes again.

"Well, spot on there, my boy. And do you know that Lady Williams did everything she could to restore the marriage after that and was madder than a hornet when her dearest and best friend scooped him up instead?"

"No, I did not. Pray tell, how is it you know that?"

"My dear boy, people tell you all sorts of things when you walk around with your collar on backwards. But I thought you should hear the sordid tale of Leon and Mary and Gwen."

"Carry on. What else do you know?"

"I hear you met with Madame Maria de la Sauvée."

"I have."

"Did you know that she is also one of Leon-the-lion-hunter's paramours?"

"Edward! Really!" his wife said.

"Margaret, darling. This is Sherlock Holmes, and he has Scotland Yard with him, and they're conducting a murder investigation. All the dirty laundry would have to come out in court anyway. Better I tell my stories from the altar rail than the witness box."

"Go on, please, Vicar," said Holmes.

"Madame is an excellent writer and also dreamed of publishing a small but critically acclaimed periodical. She tried to do so a decade ago."

"I did not know that. What happened."

"She found some brilliant writers. The covers were splendidly eye-catching. She issued several excellent monthly editions and built her monthly sales to well over five thousand, mostly through newsagents. Flushed with success, she took the plunge. She borrowed money from her friends, and printed twenty thousand, distributed them to newsagents all over Britain, and promptly went bankrupt."

"What happened?"

"Unbeknownst to her, Lady Carrington and her minions had purchased every single copy of the earlier editions as soon as they arrived in the racks. No one else knew anything about her. All but a few copies remained unsold. She could not repay her debts, and she was utterly devastated and had no idea what had happened. Gwendolyn came along and offered her an excellent stipend to come and write for her and, having no other choice, she accepted. Her Ladyship had rescued her. It was not until several years later that someone spilled the beans and told how she had been had. She has hated Gwendolyn with a passion ever since."

"Enough to murder her?"

"And more."

"Enough not to care if Mildred Smith also died?"

"Ah, there's the rub. No, she quite adored Mildred. And for that reason alone, I do not believe she could be your murderer, Mr. Holmes."

"Then who was?"

"Clive."

Holmes paused before responding, and I knew he was about to reach for his cigarette case and take several drafts before speaking. I gave him an elbow and whispered.

"You're in a church."

He harumphed and put the case back in his pocket.

"I assume," said Reverend Chrisparkle, "you know that Clive Clapper was her step-brother? It's a clear case of *cui bono*."

"Is that so?"

"You should know that some of the things he does after dark are against the law."

"Edward," said his wife.

"Yes, darling. But it is germane to the case, and it may lead to solving the murder. Someone is trying to blackmail Clive with the threat of exposing him to the public and forcing the removal of his beloved daughter from his custody."

"Are you certain of that?" asked Holmes. "Has he confessed to you his actions and their consequences?"

"Our clan does not do confession, Mr. Holmes, "but yes, he has spoken to me about it."

"And what did you tell him?"

"Following the example of Our Lord, I told him that neither do I condemn thee, go and sin no more. Come to think about it, I must have told him that on seventy times seven occasions. He clearly understands the first half and ignores the second."

"When we spoke to him, he claimed that he did not need the money and that he would hand over every farthing he received from Lady Carrington's estate to a literary trust."

"Mostly directed to the rehabilitation of Oscar Wilde? Is that what he claimed?"

"Yes, that is precisely what he said."

"Well, he would say that, wouldn't he? And did you believe him?"

"I had my doubts."

"And so do I, and for that reason, he remains at the top of my list."

"What about that Saxon Sydenham fellow? What was your opinion of him?"

"I had never met him before and had no idea what he was doing there. He has never been a member of Gwendolyn's stable. Beyond that, I found him somewhat—"

"Edward," his wife interrupted again. "You do not know the man, and you mustn't be uncharitable."

"Yes, darling, I would never think of it. And yes, Mr. Holmes, speaking charitably, I did not like the man at all. I found him oily and smarmy—the type of fellow that you shake hands with and then count your fingers. Beyond that, I cannot see what possible connection he has to the murder."

"I take it," said Holmes, "that you are not aware that Lady Carrington sold the *Cornwall Monthly Review* to him along with all its assets."

A look of shock swept across the vicar's face. He leaned forward, placed his not insignificant weight on his forearms, causing the altar rail to bow ever so slightly.

"I did not know that, and I am surprised to hear of it. However, knowing of Lady Carrington's plans to run off to Africa with her great explorer, I must say that her doing so is not entirely incongruent with her ambitions. Ah, frailty thy name is woman. Are you certain of this, Mr. Holmes?"

"I have seen the signed Agreement. It appears to be valid, although it is also a matter of our investigation."

"Well, now, that does throw the entire matter into a different light, does it not?"

"It does indeed," said Holmes, "and as I have no further questions, we thank you for your time and shall let you return to your preparations for tomorrow."

We stood to leave, but Inspector Farber placed a hand on Holmes's wrist.

"I have some further questions," he said and did not wait for Holmes to acknowledge him.

"My questions," he said, "are directed to Mrs. Chrisparkle."

The vicar's wife looked up at him, very much surprised. He continued.

"Madam, I need to ask you something, and I do so as an Inspector for Scotland Yard and as part of a murder investigation. Anything you say will be kept in strictest confidence. I am sure you will respond frankly and truthfully."

"Well…why, surely I will, but I don't see how I can be of any help to you."

"Kindly let me be the judge of that. My first question, madam. When your husband returned from the *soirée* on Saturday evening, did he give you a full account of the event and of all of the people present?"

"Yes, he always does so for any event he attends without me."

"And did he provide you with a detailed description of Mr. Sydenham and his candid opinion of him?"

"Aye, that he did."

"Based solely on what he told you about him, what is your opinion of Mr. Sydenham?"

The woman paused and then shrugged.

"I wouldn't trust him as far as I could throw him."

"Thank you, Mrs. Chrisparkle."

Chapter Eighteen

A Beating and a Theft

Having departed St. James, Bermondsey, the three of us parted from each other. Inspector Farber fetched a cab for Scotland Yard. I returned to my surgery for the remainder of the day, and Holmes walked away without saying where he was going.

I returned to 221B around six o'clock that evening. Holmes appeared shortly afterward, and the two of us sat down to a quiet supper, thoughtfully prepared as always by the indefatigable Mrs. Hudson. On two occasions, I attempted to engage him in conversation, but he indicated that he would rather be alone with his thoughts, and I gave up.

We had finished dessert when a rather furious set of knocks came to the Baker Street door.

"I'll get it," I shouted to Mrs. Hudson, and I clambered down the stairs. A bicycle boy who was panting for breath thrust an envelope into my hand. I gave him the standard fee, shut the door, and turned and began to mount the stairs. I recognized the handwriting on the envelope and hastened to tear it open as I climbed. I sat back down as I began to read.

A minute later, I thrust the note at Holmes and shouted.

"We have to go! Now! Please, Holmes, I need you to come with me."

He read the note and leapt to his feet. "Fetch your service revolver," he said. "I will meet you on the pavement."

The handwritten note was from Miss Mildred Smith, and it ran:

Dearest John:

I need your help. If at all possible, could you and Mr. Holmes please come immediately to Lady Carrington's house? I have been badly beaten, and the house has been robbed. Thank you in advance. I remain, yours truly, Millie.

I ran up to my bedroom, pulled out my revolver, loaded the bullets, and bounded back down the two flights of stairs to Baker Street. Holmes had already hailed a cab, and we jumped inside.

I shouted the address to the driver and added, "And a pound more if you will get us there quickly!"

"Right you are there, sir!" he shouted back and laid his whip to the hindquarters of his horse. The traffic on London's streets had cleared for the day, and he was able to canter the horse most of the way, urging it into a gallop whenever an open stretch of road appeared in front of us.

As a rule, I had learned not to allow my feelings to enter into any case in which I assisted Sherlock Holmes. This case was an exception. My stomach was in knots. As we tore through the center of London and across Waterloo Bridge, I could not help being consumed with worry and kept peering out the cab window to see if we were almost there.

When I looked over at Holmes, he was sitting placidly, almost serene.

"Who could have done this?" I said to him, far more loudly than was necessary.

"I do not yet know, my friend," he said. "However, I must say that this case is becoming increasingly complicated and thus more challenging. Not at all a run-of-the-mill murder case. I am beginning to enjoy it."

"Enjoy it?! Holmes, an innocent woman was almost murdered and has now been beaten. How can you say you are enjoying it?" I admit, I was more than just peeved with him.

"My dear Watson, she is not only still alive but sufficiently clear-headed to write you a note. She seems a healthy sort, and I am sure she will recover soon. I certainly hope she will. We need her to come to Cornwall with us tomorrow morning."

I said nothing more until the cab stopped on Bermondsey Wall Road. A police wagon was parked in front of Lady Carrington's home, and a constable was standing at the front door. I leapt out of the cab, slammed far more than the required fare into the driver's outstretched hand and ran toward the house.

"Are you Doctor Watson," said the constable as he blocked my way through the door.

"Yes! Now kindly let me through!"

He stepped aside. "The lady said to let you in. She's in one of the bedrooms upstairs."

I hurried through the hallway and up the stairs, taking two or three steps at a time. I assumed, correctly, that Millie would be in the same bedroom as she had been a week ago. I was right. In what had been Dr. Sterndale's private boudoir, she was once again lying in the bed, propped up by several pillows and attended to by Mrs. Sheridan.

Even from across the room, I could see the large goose egg on her forehead and the dark patch over her left eye. The eye was swollen shut.

I rushed to her side.

"Millie, are you injured. Do I need to get you to hospital?"

Mrs. Sheridan answered.

"No, Doctor, you do not. I have examined her already, and other than the bump on her head, her black eye and a nasty scratch on her throat, there is nothing wrong with her, and she is free now to get up and move around as long as she does not exert herself."

I looked down at the patient. "Can you get up? Do you need help?"

"Oh, John," she said. "I knew you would come. Thank you. I am so sorry that I look such a mess. I truly did not want you to see me like this, but you were the one man I knew I could call on. Thank you, John."

She moved her gaze from me to the door of the room as Sherlock Holmes entered. He gazed around the room and walked slowly over to the bed.

"Please state what happened," he said to Millie. "There is no need for edited eloquence. Just the facts, madam."

She took several deep breaths and then pulled her legs up, swung them around, sat on the edge of the bed and looked directly at Holmes.

"I was alone in the house all day. I came here directly after having met with you this morning. I was trying to put all the records of the *Review* in order with the hope and prayer that there might be some way found to keep it going. Around four o'clock, there was a knock on the door. I answered it and that man … what's his name? … Saxon something—"

"Mr. Sydenham?" I said.

"Yes, him. He told me that he was here to remove all of the assets and records of the *Cornwall Monthly Review*. I was shocked by what he said, and I let him know in no uncertain terms that he had no right to do anything of the kind and ordered him out of the house. He thrust a set of papers into my face and demanded that I read them. It was the

Agreement with Lady Carrington of her sale of everything to him. The papers said—"

"We have read them, madam," said Holmes. "Please continue."

"Yes, yes, of course. Dr. Watson had told me about them. Well, I read them, and I saw where it said that we had until Monday to turn over everything to him. So, I told him that he had no right to anything until then and to leave. He pushed himself past me, and I tried to stop him."

"You physically attempted to stop him?" said Holmes.

"Oh, I know. I was foolish. He is a big, powerful man. I was not thinking, but I was so angry that I started kicking him, slapping him…anything I could do to stop him. I landed a solid left hook on his jaw."

"Did he hit you back?"

"Oh, yes. He delivered a good one. Let me have it in the eye with his fist. Knocked me off my feet, and I landed head first on the floor."

"That beast!" I exclaimed. "What sort of a man would—,"

"Please, Watson. Save the indignation for later. Now, madam, what happened after that?"

"I staggered to my feet, and I was furious. I came at him, ready to bite or scratch his eyes out. But he was ready for me. He spun me around and put his arm around my neck. He was holding a knife, and then he covered my face with a handkerchief that was soaked in chloroform. I passed out."

"For how long?" said Holmes.

"It must have been well over an hour. The maid says she returned at half-past five and that she ran down the street to Mrs. Sheridan's house and got her to come immediately."

"And what time," said Holmes to Mrs. Sheridan, "did you arrive?"

"At fifteen minutes to six," the older woman replied. "Miss Smith was just regaining consciousness, and the maid and I helped her up to this bedroom. As soon as she was coherent, she insisted on writing a note to Dr. Watson, and the maid took it down to the street and found a bicycle boy to deliver it."

"I am glad we were at home to receive the note," said Holmes, "and to come forthwith."

"But you're too late," said Millie.

"I beg your pardon, miss," said Holmes.

"You're too late. He took everything. I had all the submissions—an entire year's worth—all sorted and filed and put in a steamer trunk, and all the writers' and printers' contracts, and the subscription lists, and the newsagents' addresses…everything. He took it all."

Holmes said nothing for a minute and then turned to Mrs. Sheridan.

"Would you mind," he asked her, "staying with Miss Smith until, in your judgment, she can be left alone? Dr. Watson and I have other matters to attend to."

"I will do that, Mr. Holmes."

"Thank you. Now, Watson. Come, we have a call to make."

"To Saxon what's-his-name?"

"Yes."

Holmes turned and strode quickly out of the room, down the hall and down the stairs. I gave a quick goodbye wave to Millie and hurried after him.

He stopped in the hallway and looked around.

"This is where she was assaulted," he said.

I noticed that one of the chairs was out of place but nothing else.

Holmes dropped to his knees and reached under another chair and procured a white handkerchief. He held it to his nose and then handed it over to me. I did likewise.

"It's chloroform, all right," I said.

"Indeed, it is, with a faint scent of men's cologne." He took it back from me, sniffed it again, looked puzzled for a moment, and stuffed it in his pocket.

"It is only a block to Sydenham's. We can walk faster than waiting for a cab. Let us be off."

He moved out and continued at the pace of a forced march until we rounded the block to the street in which the house was located. Then we stopped.

In front of the Sydenham house, there were two police carriages. A half-dozen uniformed constables stood on the pavement, blocking the way of a small crowd of neighbors.

"Good heavens," I said. "What is going on there?"

Chapter Nineteen

Shot by a Large Man

"We are about to find out," said Holmes.

We approached the house, and Holmes identified himself to one of the constables.

"Right, Mr. Holmes," said the policeman. "That was fast. The inspectors will be happy to see you."

We entered the house, and another constable called out. "Inspector, sir. Mr. Holmes is here!"

Inspector Lestrade, followed by Inspector Farber, came out of the parlor and met us in the hallway.

"Well, you were quick, Holmes. I only just sent a man to fetch you ten minutes ago. And that tells me that he never saw you and that you are here of your own accord and that you better tell me all you know about a man lying in the parlor with a bullet through his back."

"Mr. Saxon Sydenham is dead?" said Holmes.

"That's the usual condition of men who have a bullet through them. Here, take a look."

Lying face-down on the carpet in the parlor was Saxon Sydenham. He was clad in his elegant dressing gown, linen shirt, and leather slippers. In the middle of his back, just to the left of his spine, was a dark circle of blood.

"He was shot in the back," I said.

"That's right, Doctor," said Lestrade. "At first we thought someone had stood in the garden right outside the window and shot him at close range. But there are no marks of anything thing being disturbed. No footprints. Nothing. And he was not shot with a revolver. Someone got him with a rifle."

"How do you know that?" asked Holmes.

"It's called basic police work, Mr. Holmes. First we see that there is another bullet lodged in the wall right here."

He pointed to a spot in the wall where the plaster had been carved out.

"And we see that it's from a thirty-caliber rifle. So, we deduce that whoever shot him stood across the road, hidden in that clump of trees. The victim may have been sitting on his sofa or somewhere else in the room. So, the killer shot through the open window and landed a bullet in the wall. Mr. Sydenham gets up to see why his wall is exploding and *bang*, he gets it in the back. My men checked out those trees, and, as I expected, there's some footprints, and we've already ordered up a plaster-of-paris cast to be made."

Holmes turned and looked out the window.

"Those trees are at least a hundred and fifty feet away. Whoever fired the shots must have been a very skilled marksman."

"And he might have something to do with the murder a week ago of Lady Carrington. Is that right, Holmes?"

"We have insufficient data at this time to make that conclusion."

"Is that right? Well, Inspector Farber here tells me that you and he met with the deceased just yesterday concerning the Carrington murder, and today he turns up dead, and you turn up before you knew I sent for you. So that says maybe there is sufficient data, as you call it, to form a hypothesis, as you call it. So how about you tell me all you know about who could have killed Lady Carrington and who might also want this fellow here dead."

As the constables went about their work, and the medical officers removed the body from the house, Sherlock Holmes shared with Inspector Lestrade all of the information and insights he had acquired to date. Much of what he said was confirmed by Inspector Farber, who had been present at the interviews. When he had concluded, Lestrade gave him a hard look.

"Right, then who amongst this unsavory lot is your primary suspect?"

"I cannot say. Perhaps our visit to Cornwall will shed additional light. I will be happy to report to you on Monday."

We bade farewell to the inspectors and stepped out on to the pavement. I started to hail a cab when Holmes caught my arm.

"Give me two minutes," he said, and then he walked quickly across the road to the clump of trees where a constable was busy taking impressions of the footprints. He stood still and looked at the ground for somewhat more than two minutes and then came back to the cab I had meanwhile secured for us.

Once inside and on our way, I turned to Holmes.

"Distinct footprints?" I asked.

"Of a large man, walking slowly."

"Is it not obvious who must have fired that shot?"

"Nothing, my dear Doctor, about this case is obvious. However, before we get very far, might I ask you to stop off at Lady Carrington's house and check and make sure that Miss Smith is prepared to travel with us tomorrow morning. I'm sure you would not mind doing so."

He winked at me.

"Happy to do so," I said and grinned back.

Mildred Smith was alone in Lady Carrington's house and greeted me at the door. Her bruises were looking rather nasty, but she welcomed me inside.

"John, please don't ask me to open the curtains or turn up the lamps. I took a look at myself in the mirror, and I look hideous. It upsets me to think of you looking at me in this condition."

I protested, but nevertheless, the lamps stayed low, and we chatted briefly over a glass of Lady Carrington's excellent brandy. I opened a fresh bottle, not forgetting what had happened to a previous bottle of Port. This time around, she accepted my offer to escort her to her home, and we walked, with her taking my arm, to a row of modest houses adjacent to Southwark Park.

"I would love to ask you to come in, John," she said. "But both of us have to be at Paddington at seven tomorrow morning, and it would be best if we were rested and ready for whatever Mr. Sherlock Holmes has in store for us."

I agreed, and this time I took the initiative and kissed her goodnight.

Chapter Twenty

Alone with Millie

addington was about twenty-five minutes' walk from 221B Baker Street, and, it being a pleasant June morning, Holmes and I set out at twenty-past six, carrying our small overnight valises. On arriving, Holmes purchased the tickets for three passengers through to Penzance and handed two of them to me.

"I have booked two first-class cabins, a separate one for myself and a different one for you and Miss Smith. I fear that the two of you will chatter all the way to Cornwall, making it impossible for me to concentrate."

A wisp of a smile flashed across his face, and I grinned back.

"An excellent move," I said. "It would never do to interrupt your concentration."

At five minutes to seven, Miss Mildred Smith appeared on the platform, a porter following her with her baggage. The damage done to her face the previous afternoon was now almost impossible to see, at least from a distance. She had arranged her hair so that the goose egg was covered by a swoop of curls that fell down over her forehead, and she had applied a layer of cosmetic face powder over her blackened eye.

"Good morning, gentlemen," she said. "What a pleasant prospect for a June morning. I am looking forward to several hours of travel with two wonderful men, and all I ask is that you do not look too closely at me. This was the best I could do with my appearance under the circumstances."

Holmes said nothing, but I said, "You look quite smashing."

"Oh, John, you are such a liar, and I thank you."

We boarded, and I felt an impish sense of glee when it became apparent that Millie and I would have a cabin all to ourselves whilst Holmes had to share his with a mother and her three children.

Over the next six hours, the two of us divided our time between effortless conversation and reading. As first-class passengers, we twice exercised the privilege of moving through the corridor from our cabin back to the restaurant car. About three hours into the journey, as we pulled out of Exeter, Millie put down the novel she was reading and asked if I would do the same. I complied, wondering what was on her mind.

"John, my dear, I have somewhat to say unto thee about the stories you have written and published in the *Strand*."

"Do you now? And what do you have to tell me about them?"

"I feel it is my duty as an experienced editor to offer some suggestions."

"Jolly, good. As you are one of the finest editors in the Empire, I welcome your advice."

"John, you really must stop making such ridiculous mistakes and blunders in your stories."

"Mistakes? What mistakes?"

"Let us start with *A Study in Scarlet*. The geographical location of the Great Alkali Plain is simply and impossibly wrong. There is no such arid and repulsive desert in the place you say it is. The Pawnees and the Blackfeet Indian tribes do not live anywhere near there. The man you call 'The Prophet,' who we all know was Brigham Young, could not possibly have been leading a massive train of ten thousand Mormons on the fourth of May, 1847. The angel who gave the golden plates to Joseph Smith was named *Moroni*, never anything else, and certainly never *Merona*. Gold fever did not recently break out in California in 1859. It had broken out in 1849, ten years earlier, and had long passed. The gold rush of 1859 was in Colorado and of much less significance, and in Nevada, they were mining for silver, not gold."

I was, I admit, somewhat taken aback but mumbled something to the effect of, "Oh, yes, well, jolly good. I'll have my editor attend to those in the next edition."

I picked up the novel I had been reading and returned my attention to its pages.

"John, I am far from finished. In your *Red-Headed League* story, six months disappear in the middle of the story. You begin Mr. Wilson's ordeal in April, and it magically ends in October. And surely, you cannot expect any intelligent reader to believe that snakes could be trained to respond to a whistle, let alone slither down a bell-rope. And about your dear wife—may she rest in peace. Did she have a mother in England or not? In *The Sign of the Four,* you tell us that her mother was dead, but in *The Five Orange Pips,* she was on a visit to her mother— the mother who has been dead for some time. And John, in what part of your body were you shot with a Jezail bullet? Was it your shoulder or your leg? You really must make up your mind. And honestly, John, was Mary Morstan so dim-witted that she could not remember her husband's name? She married John Watson, not James."

She paused for a moment, allowing me to respond.

"Right, I'll have those corrections made. You have a keen editor's eye. Anything else?"

"Yes. Whatever happened to your bull pup?"

"I left him with one of the other guests at the private hotel in the *Strand*. Holmes did not object to him, but Mrs. Hudson was having no part of it. I'm not at all sure how long I can keep Pilot."

This time I deliberately picked up my novel and started to read again. From that time until we arrived in Penzance, we kept our conversation to reading each other passages of note in our respective books.

The hour of one in the afternoon had passed by the time we arrived at the Penzance station. It had been three years since Holmes and I had been in this far portion of the Cornish peninsula, and my memory of the horror we had witnessed was still fresh. Nevertheless, I hoped that our visit this time would be more congenial.

After checking our baggage with the station master, we walked along the edge of the harbor to the solicitor's office. The view out to the ocean was rather stunning.

"This solicitor," said Holmes, "is not accustomed to working on a Saturday afternoon, but because of your sensational stories about me, Watson, he was eager to meet even if it meant giving up his golf game for one day."

It was no more than four blocks from the station to the offices of Clouded, Waddlers, and Proodes, the firm that, for years, had handled all matters of titles, conveyances, wills and estates for the Carrington family. A young solicitor, thin, spectacled and eager, was waiting at the door to welcome us.

He had his card at the ready and handed one to me and to Holmes.

"Miss Smith would like to receive your card as well," I said, trying to sound mildly annoyed.

"Oh, yes, of course. Terribly sorry Miss, but I only brought two from my desk."

"We can wait until you fetch one," I said. He gave me a bit of a look but retreated back into the office and reappeared a minute later, bearing a third card which he handed to Millie, making a bit of a show of bowing toward her. He looked up at her and appeared to stare at what was left of her goosebump and black eye.

"My name," he said, turning to Holmes, "is Mr. Willie Nailer, and I have been assigned the responsibility of looking after all matters related to the Carrington estate. Allow me to say how shocked, how utterly horrified, we were to hear of her death. Please convey our condolences to her family. And allow me also to say how pleased we are to have the opportunity of assisting the work of Mr. Sherlock Holmes."

"I am likewise pleased to assist in the investigation," said Holmes. "As you were informed in my telegram, I am acting under the authority of Scotland Yard, and I trust that there will be no impediments to my examining any and all documents I request."

"None at all, Mr. Holmes. Allow me to invite you into our board room. I have already set out all the files I thought you could possibly be interested in. You are free to go through them to your heart's content. It being a Saturday, I am the only member of the firm present, but I shall do my utmost to expedite your wishes."

He led us into a finely furnished room in which there was a large oak table, sufficient in size to accommodate a dozen people sitting around it. Spread out on the table were at least twenty separate piles of files. Each of them had a small tented cardboard card on top of it that bore the name of the contents of the pile. Most dealt with specific properties in and around Penzance and Mount's Bay, and two were labeled with the name of the tin mines that were owned by the estate. The thickest pile had the name of *Cornwall Monthly Review* attached to it. The thinnest two were *Last Will and Testament* and *Consolidated Statements*. Two others caught my immediate attention. One read *Mr. Clive Clapper* and the other *Dr. Leon Sterndale*. There was no file tagged with the name of Saxon Sydenham.

"We shall," said Holmes, "divide and conquer. We are not particularly concerned about the properties and the tin mines, but Miss Smith, might I prevail upon you to examine the files related to the *Review* and note anything that strikes you as of singular or untoward interest. Watson, kindly look at what is written about Mr. Clapper, and

I shall investigate our dear Dr. Sterndale. Having done all that, we can examine the estate statements and the Will."

.

Chapter Twenty-One

Mr. Nailer Nails It

We sat down around the table, and Mr. Nailer scurried to distribute the piles of files in accordance with the directions Holmes had given, and then he took a seat at the far end of the table. He seemed disappointed that we wished to examine only a small portion of all the work he had prepared.

I quickly scanned the files pertaining to Clive Clapper. They contained correspondence from Clapper's father, Lord Carrington, to his mother, acknowledging his paternity and his commitment to financial support. There were notes from father to son confirming arrangements for his schooling and then, after what I assumed was the death of Lord Carrington, letters back and forth between Lady Gwendolyn Carrington and Clive Clapper.

The tone of the correspondence between brother and sister was decidedly cool but not overly antagonistic. The only surprising entry in the files was the detailed information about a trust that Lady Carrington had established for the schooling of her niece, Miss Felicity Clapper.

As I handled one file after another, I looked across the table several times at Millie. She was thumbing through her files in a desultory manner but glancing intermittently at the file labeled *Last Will and Testament.*

I put the last file back on top of the pile and leaned back in my chair. Within a minute, Holmes and Millie did likewise.

"Anything of interest?" Holmes asked, and I told him about the trust for Clapper's daughter.

Millie shrugged. "Nothing here. There is naught in these files except copies of all the contracts and correspondence I wrote and signed on behalf of the *Review*—only items I wrote myself and sent copies down to the solicitor here in Penzance."

"And you, Holmes?" I asked. "The Sterndale file was rather thin, and so I deduce the contents were recent."

"An excellent deduction, Watson. All of the documents were related to the purchase by Lady Carrington of properties from Dr. Sterndale."

"That took place," chimed in Mr. Nailer, "just over a year ago. Our firm handled all of the transactions, registrations and conveyances for Lady Carrington."

"Yes, I see that in the file," said Holmes. "And what advice did you give Lady Carrington concerning the price she paid?"

The young man looked somewhat nonplussed. "I'm … I'm sorry Mr. Holmes, but the advice we give to our clients is protected by—,"

"By nothing whatsoever," said Holmes, "when an investigation into a murder is taking place. Now, you can either answer my questions freely and frankly in the comfort of your office, or I can have a constable escort you to the local station, and you can be interrogated there. The choice is yours."

The poor fellow was turning red in the face, and he looked toward the door as if hoping against hope that one of the senior partners of the firm might have come into the office by chance on a Saturday and could come to his rescue. Seeing no such relief, he stumbled through an answer.

"We advised Lady Carrington that we believed she was paying far too high a price, and we urged her not to carry out the sale."

"And in your opinion and that of your colleagues in this firm, why would she do such a thing?"

"I can only speak for myself, sir—,"

"No, young man, you most certainly had discussions with other members of this firm, and they voiced their opinions. What did they say?"

He took a deep breath and looked ill at ease but soldiered on.

"This Dr. Sterndale fellow, sir. Do you know him?"

"I do," said Holmes.

"He is quite the forceful character, if I may say so."

"I agree entirely. Continue."

"He seemed to be able to exert considerable influence over Lady Carrington. Speaking frankly, sir, we all thought he was controlling her."

"I am not surprised by what you say. However, it is not as if she would be financially injured by paying a thousand pounds more than the property was worth. She would hardly miss it. What else was wrong with the transaction?"

"There was some question concerning the title to the property Dr. Sterndale was selling her. Are you aware, sir, that Dr. Sterndale has a wife?"

"You are referring to Lady Mary Williams?"

Mr. Nailer looked a bit surprised and then smirked. "I suppose I should not be shocked that Sherlock Holmes knows things. So, yes, sir, the title to some of Dr. Sterndale's properties are held jointly by himself and his wife, and other properties are solely in her name. He did not have the right to sell them without her written agreement."

"Then, in your capacity as Lady Carrington's solicitors, what did you do?"

"We privately contacted Lady Williams and sent her a complete record of the proposed sales and purchases and asked her to send an affidavit confirming her consent."

"And did you receive it back?"

"Well, yes and no, Mr. Holmes."

"Explain."

"She appeared in our office a few days later, bearing a signed consent document."

"Then what is the problem?"

"Our firm has handled many of her affairs in the past as well, and we have her signature on file. It appeared that someone had forged her signature. We could not prove that, and she was standing there handing it to us, so we accepted it. And please, Mr. Holmes, if you can make any sense of it all, kindly tell me because all of us here are as blind as moles trying to sort it out."

Holmes closed his eyes, leaned back in his chair, and tented his fingertips in front of his sternum. For a long minute, he said nothing, but his head was moving ever so slightly back and forth and up and down, and his lips quivered as if he were carrying on a conversation with himself.

Mr. Nailer looked utterly bewildered and was about to say something when I held my finger against my lips and bade him, "Ssshhh."

Holmes's head and lips stopped moving. A slow smile appeared. He opened his eyes and spoke to Mr. Nailer.

"By chance, when Lady Williams was here, did she also happen to meet briefly with a member of your firm who takes on criminal cases?"

"Why, yes, she did. Before departing, she met for a few minutes with Mr. Kaiser Drake. He handles criminal defense."

"And what did she ask, and what did he tell her? And do not even think about protesting client confidentiality."

"She asked him about the penalties for anyone convicted of carrying out fraud and forgery in the sale and purchase of property. And Kaiser told her that the courts take property crime very seriously and anyone convicted could face several years in prison."

"As I expected. Thank you, Mr. Nailer. Now then, let us turn to Lady Carrington's Will."

Chapter Twenty-Two

Where There is a Will

Before Holmes could retrieve the file bearing the Will, Mr. Nailer was on his feet and scampered to fetch it and hand it to him. Holmes thanked him, opened the file, and held the document up in front of himself.

"Can you confirm, sir," he said to the solicitor, "that this is an authentic document? Was it signed in your presence?"

"Not in mine, sir, but she came in here and instructed us to dispose of her previous Will and prepare this one. She signed it in front of Mr. Waddlers himself. He witnessed it."

"Excellent, then let us take a look at what it says. Yes, as expected, *Know all persons by these presents that I Gwendolyn Ottoline Carrington being of sound mind* …and so on and so on. She names her family, which is limited to *Clive Merryweather Clapper, step-brother and illegitimate son of Lord Caldwell Carrington and Niece, Felicity Filomena Clapper* …and that's the lot. Now then let me move ahead several Articles to … yes, here it is. *I give, devise and bequeath unto* … and there is a long list."

He turned to Mr. Nailer. "Have notices been sent to the beneficiaries?"

"Not yet, sir. When the death occurs under suspicious circumstances of any sort, we do not rush to notify them."

"Of course not. Well then, I see that she bequeathed her tin mines and the Carrington Manor home over by Longrock to her brother, Clive Clapper, but it has some conditions added."

"It's a *fideicommissum* clause, Mr. Holmes," said Willie Nailer. "He gets the house and the mines but only on the condition that he uses the income from the mines to maintain the house and the immediate property, and he must, in turn, bequeath them to his daughter. Her Ladyship wanted to make sure the old home remained in the family."

"Quite so. Next, she instructs her executor to liquidate all of her assets and disperse the cash in the following manner to all those on the list. Let's see. There is a substantial bequest to the RSPCA, very large bequests to Lady Cavendish College and Newnham College at Cambridge for the endowing of a Carrington Chair of Creative Writing and bursaries to be awarded to deserving and promising young women. Then we have two pages of the names of numerous hospitals and charities, and one small one item at the end. She wants one thousand pounds given to whoever takes care of her dog, Pilot, to be used for his care and feeding."

He put the document back on the table. I looked at the signature lines.

"The witness is Reverend Roundhay. You remember him, don't you, Holmes?"

"Certainly, I do. Perhaps we should call on him. I should not be surprised to find that he has some insights into what all has gone on here."

"I'm sure he would have," said Mr. Nailer. "But unfortunately, he passed away a few months ago."

"Oh, no," I said. "I am saddened to hear that. He was a fine fellow."

"Do not be too sad, Watson, my friend," said Holmes. "You are in luck. You have one thousand pounds coming your way because you agreed to look after that mangy old spaniel."

I was about to reply, but Millie spoke first. Her voice was trembling. "Is that all?"

"Yes, Miss Smith," said Holmes. "That's all there is. There isn't any more."

"Nothing about a trust to keep the *Review* going?"

"Not a word."

"But she told me she had put it in her Will. She said she added a footnote, a … what do you call it?"

"A *codicil,* miss," said Nailer.

"Yes. She told me she had added a codicil." Her voice was trembling.

"There is none there, Miss," said Nailer.

"Is this … is this the only copy of her Will? Is there another one anywhere?"

"We did make a copy, miss. Two, in fact. Either she took them back with her to London, or they are kept out at the Carrington Manor."

"We have to go there!" said Millie. "I know they're not in London. They must be out at the manor. We have to go. She told me she had set up a trust. She promised me!"

She was now sounding desperate. Her face was contorted, and her fists clenched. Tears were forming in her eyes. Instinctively, I responded.

"Certainly, we can. We can go there straight away, can't we, Holmes?"

He did not seem overly eager, but I insisted. "If there is a second Will, we need to make certain that it says the same as this one. The courts will require it."

Holmes sighed. "Very well, then. Where is this manor house?"

"The Carrington Manor, sir," said Nailer, "is only a half-hour down the coast toward Poldhu Bay. Shall I guide you there?"

"Thank you, but that will not be necessary. Dr. Watson and I are familiar with the road from a previous visit."

We stood and prepared to leave the room, but we stopped by Mr. Nailer.

"Mr. Holmes. There is one more thing that I have to tell you."

"What is that?"

"It's about Dr. Sterndale."

"What about him?"

"He's here. He came by our office around eleven o'clock this morning. The door was open, and he entered, and he found me here."

"What did he want?"

"He had some questions about making sure that the sale of his property was not going to be impeded by the death of Lady Carrington."

"It is understandable that he would have that concern. But as we did not come to investigate him, and he does not know that we are here, I cannot see why you are so distraught in telling me about him, as you clearly are."

"He does know that you're here, sir."

"He does? How?"

The fellow was now looking down at the floor, and in just above a whisper, he said, "Because I told him."

"You what!" said Holmes.

"I'm sorry, Mr. Holmes. I'm terribly sorry. It was just that I was so chuffed about being entrusted by the firm to meet with Sherlock Holmes and do so all by myself, that I was bursting to tell someone. I guess I was bragging a little, and I let it out during the course of my conversation with him."

"And how did he react?"

"He was not pleased, sir. And Mr. Holmes, sir, Dr. Sterndale is well-known down here in Cornwall and, frankly, feared. He is a volatile man, and I have to warn you to be on a careful watch for him."

"Thank you for doing so. And thank you too for all the fine work you did to prepare for our visit. Greatly appreciated."

He gave the young man a friendly clap on his shoulder, and we departed from the building.

"That," I said to him, "was awfully decent of you. I would think you would be furious with him for what he disclosed to Sterndale."

"Not at all, my dear Watson. Not at all. Having one of our suspects close by and watching us means that we can also be watching him. That is far more efficient than having him back in London."

"Ah, so you do consider him a suspect."

"One of several, yes. Come now, we should be able to find a driver at the station that will take us out to the Carrington estate."

As we walked back up to the station, Millie took my arm and, with her free hand, held on to me. Twice, I feared she was going to collapse.

She smiled and, in a weak voice, said, "I'm so sorry, John. I'm finding this much more difficult than I expected. I cannot tell you how grateful I am that you are here with me."

Chapter Twenty-Three

Safe in the Manor

At the station, we contracted with a local livery service to drive us out to the Carrington Manor. On a calm summer day, the sinister semicircle of Mounts Bay, that old death trap of sailing vessels, with its fringe of black cliffs, creaming breakers and surge-swept reefs on which innumerable seamen have met their end, was deceptively picturesque.

Millie had recovered her spirits and was approaching serenity as she gazed out over the ocean.

"I spent several years living here," she said, "and I never got tired of the view of the ocean. I have not had that opportunity for some time now. It's good to be back."

Her improved spirit was contagious, and I relaxed and enjoyed the splendor of Cornwall's rugged coast.

Holmes did not. For the entire distance, he was either scowling or sitting with his eyes closed and his jaw firmly set.

It only took us a half-hour to arrive at the narrow road that led up the sloping coastal plain to the manor. The house had a commanding view of the bay and the vast western mouth of the English Channel beyond. In keeping with the style of the region, the house was a large Tudor building with three floors and numerous windows, all consisting of diamond-shaped leaded glass. Trees had been planted along each side of the house and in clumps behind it, but the grounds in front held nothing but flowers and lawn. Nothing diminished the stunning vista.

As we pulled up to the door, a maid and a man-servant came running out of the house to greet us—more specifically, to greet Miss Mildred Smith.

"Millie!" sang the maid. "How lovely to see you here. Thank you for coming, dearie. We have been at our wits' end since hearing the news of Her Ladyship."

"Aye," chimed in the man-servant. "The beautiful face of a sensible woman is a godsend. And who might your two gentlemen friends be, Millie, my dear?"

He extended his hand and helped Millie step down from the carriage.

"They are more than just gentlemen friends, Alex, you silver-tongued old sailor. May I introduce you and Miss Bertha to Mr. Sherlock Holmes and Dr. Watson."

"Crivvens! They have turned the big guns on us. If Sherlock Holmes hisself is investigating Her Ladyship's death, something more than burthensack is going on. Well then, welcome to Carrington Manor, gentlemen."

Although the exterior of the house would lead one to believe it was built several centuries ago, the interior was surprisingly modern in design. Electric lighting had been installed throughout, and the furniture was of the finest quality and taste as one could expect to find in Mayfair.

The fellow Millie called Alex offered to give Holmes and me a tour of the house, and I would not have minded seeing it, but Millie intervened.

"No, Alex, my dear," she said, "we are on urgent business. We have to inspect Lady Carrington's files and look for documents that might give Mr. Sherlock Holmes some insights into her murder."

"Auch, well, you know where her desk was. Take your gents and have a look."

We followed her into a small study at the back of the house. It was lined with what may have been original paintings by Constable, Turner, and Gainsborough, many *objets d'art* and a handful of leatherbound books. There was a desk in the corner, and Millie rushed to it immediately and pulled open the lower drawers. From them, she extracted an armful of files.

"This is where she kept everything important. At least she did when I lived and worked here."

We divided up the trove, and for the next hour, we perused the contents. There were numerous copies of documents related to properties, many of them signed by Mrs. Sheridan but nothing that resembled a Will.

Millie had become increasingly tense and was almost feverishly flipping page after page and uttering sighs of exasperation.

"It's not here!" she cried. "But I know there has to be another copy. ALEX! Can you help us?"

The man entered the room and courteously asked what the problem was, and Millie sputtered out her frustration with not being able to find what we were looking for.

"It would be in her safe," he said.

"What safe?" demanded Millie.

"Aye, she acquired one a few years ago. It's in her dressing room. Come. I'll show ye."

We followed him up the stairs and into an airy, spacious room, graced by a large expanse of window that afforded a magnificent view out over the ocean. The adjacent room was filled with racks of clothes and shelves of shoes and boots. Stuck back in a corner was a small block-shaped safe, about two feet square, and having a rather ornate design.

"She bought that from the Morgans when they sold off and moved to America," said Alex.

"Do you happen to know the combination?" I asked.

"Auch, mon. I canna help ye with that. Her ladyship was the only one. Aye, and old man Morgan would still remember it. He's in Florida, I heard. We could send off a wire and try to find him."

Millie gasped. "We haven't time for that. We have to find the Will and get back to London by Monday."

"Holmes," I said, looking at my friend. "Can you—"

"I can. If the lot of you will leave and allow me an hour of silence, I should be able to open it."

Over the next hour, Millie took my arm, and we strolled around the lovely front lawn and gardens of the estate and stopped numerous times to look out over the water. It was now late in the afternoon but, it being the solstice, the sun was still well above the horizon and giving the entire coastline a golden hue. After five o'clock had passed, we returned to the house and had tea with Alex and Bertha. They had noticed the remnants of the goose egg and black eye on Millie's face and, when she caught them stealing glances at her, she hastened to explain. They were horrified to hear first about the attack on her and, when I took over the story, of the murder of her attacker.

They were also understandably concerned about the future ownership of the estate, and I was able to pass along to them what we had witnessed in the Will that Lady Carrington had left with her solicitor.

"Auch, so Clive will take it over, will he?" said Alex. "What do you think of that, Bertha?"

"He's a bit of a pompous twit, but no so bad. His bark is worse than his bite. He's come down here a few times every year and brought the girl with him."

"Aye," said Alex, "and isn't she a piece of work. Every time I see them together, it proves to me that there is a God in heaven, and your sins will find you out."

Bertha laughed and started into anecdotes about Clive and his daughter that I found amusing, but I could sense Millie becoming more and more tense as the minutes ticked by.

"Should we go and check on Mr. Holmes?" she asked.

"No," I said. "He'll come down in his own good time."

When another half-hour had passed, I changed my mind.

"Perhaps," I said, "we can bring him a cup of tea and a biscuit or two. He might like that."

Bertha organized a tray, and I carried it upstairs to the bedroom. Holmes was sitting cross-legged on the floor with his ear pressed against the safe and a notebook and pencil on the floor in front of him.

He graciously thanked us for the tea and stood up, unbent his body, and accepted the cup and saucer.

"The first three numbers came quickly," he said. "Forty-six, fifteen, forty-six. But the fourth number is the devil. I have tried and tried again for nearly an hour, but I cannot hear anything. We may be here all night."

He took a sip of his tea, put the cup and saucer down on the dresser, and took a bite of a biscuit that I was quite sure had been freshly baked a week ago.

"Mr. Holmes?" said Millie.

"Yes, Miss Smith."

"I do not know much at all about safes, but did not many older safes only use three numbers and not four?"

Holmes said nothing, and his face went utterly blank for the longest time. Then a faint smile appeared, and he set his partially eaten biscuit down on his saucer and dropped to his knees in front of the safe. He dialed the three numbers he had already discerned and gave the handle a hard push downwards.

It moved.

.

Chapter Twenty-Four

Ambushed After a Footnote

The safe door swung open, revealing a small stack of files.

Holmes looked up at the two of us, held his arms out with palms turned up, and shrugged.

"It was a trifle," he said, "but there is nothing so important as trifles."

He retrieved the files from the safe and stood up.

"Let us see what we have here," he said as he laid the files out on the dresser.

He rifled through them quickly and selected the one on which the words *Last Will and Testament* had been placed.

"Ah, ha," he said. "There are indeed two copies. Same date." He removed the documents and laid the pages down in front of us, one after the other. When he came to the final page, we could see that a codicil had been added in a feminine hand. He lifted the page and read.

"It says *By my hand I add this additional bequest. Upon my death, the Cornwall Monthly Review and all assets related to it, of which I am the sole owner and publisher, shall become the property of my dear friend, Lady Mary Williams and her husband, Dr. Leon Sterndale.* It is signed by Gwendolyn Ottoline Carrington and witnessed by Reverend Roland Roundhay."

Millie let out a scream of disbelief.

"Noo! It can't be! She promised it to me!"

She pushed Holmes aside and grabbed the remaining papers from the file.

"It's the other copy," she cried. "Here, look at it."

She started to toss the first pages aside, but Holmes reached over and pulled the document from her hands.

"Allow me, thank you, Miss Smith."

He laid the pages down in an orderly manner until he reached the final one. The identical codicil we had just read was on that page as well. However, it had a distinct X drawn through it, and a second codicil had been inserted. Holmes lifted the page and read.

"By my hand I revoke the above provision. I hereby instruct my executor to entrust the sum of twenty thousand pounds to the care of Hitchens, Harrison and Company with the direction that it be invested in a diversified portfolio of interest-bearing bonds and dividend-bearing stocks with the intent that the principal be preserved and that the interest and dividends earned be placed quarterly in the care of Miss Mildred Smith and used at her discretion solely for the purpose of continuing to edit and publish the Cornwall Monthly Review. All assets of the said Review shall be placed in a trust, to be likewise supervised by officers of Harrison, Hitchens and Company, and used solely for the continued operation of said Review. "

Millie shrieked with joy. "I knew it! I knew it! She promised me. I knew it had to be there. I can keep doing it. I can do it until I die."

She seemed almost delirious with joy and incoherent laughter.

"Miss Smith," said Holmes. "Control yourself. This copy has been signed by Lady Carrington and witnessed by Reverend Roundhay. The date of the codicil is November of last year. As such, it takes precedence over the two earlier copies, but there remains the contract for the sale to Saxon Sydenham. The trustee of his estate will, I expect, contest this provision. The final disposition will have to be settled by the courts."

Millie slowly staggered over to a chair and sat down. She clutched the wooden arms tightly and forced herself to breathe deeply several times. She closed her eyes and tilted her head up as if she were praying. That struck me as somewhat strange as I had assumed that she, like most emancipated, progressive, enlightened artists put little stock in the supernatural. She opened her eyes and spoke to Holmes.

"Yes, I know, Mr. Holmes, I am aware of that. But finding this copy with these words has given me hope. I feared that what I had made my life's work had been torn from my hands. My hope may still vanish, but until it does, it shall be an anchor in my soul. I trust you can understand my feelings."

Holmes said nothing, but I spoke up. "We understand entirely. We shall continue to hope with you."

"Thank you, John. And if you give me just one hour, I can collect everything I need from here for the *Review,* and then we can rush back to London straight away, can't we? There is no reason for us to stay here, is there?"

"A capital idea," I said.

"Which will not work," said Holmes. "There is no overnight train on weekends. We shall have to wait until tomorrow morning. Thus, there is no rush. I suggest that you collect such items as you consider appropriate, and Dr. Watson and I shall stroll the property and enjoy the sea air, sunshine, and patience."

"An even more capital idea," I said, and we turned and set out. Once we were out of the house and walking down the long slope toward the shore, I could not help but comment.

"Ah, isn't that grand, Holmes?"

"My dear Watson, the good Lord bestowed upon you a superb gift of silence. Pray exercise it as we walk. I have work to do inside my mind, and I cannot do it when you are making profoundly obvious statements about the scenery."

This was not the first time he had made such a comment, and I was quite sure it would not be the last. My response was to content myself with enjoying the splendor of the vista and leave him to live in the world inside his head.

In silence, we sauntered down the hill until we reached a low brick wall that marked the southern boundary of the estate. A large beech tree, planted decades ago, grew close to the wall, and the spreading roots provided a convenient step, allowing both of us to climb up to the top and enjoy an even wider panorama of the south coast of England. I climbed up first and moved a yard away from the beech tree, giving Holmes space to join me. As the two of us stood there, he extracted his beloved pipe, lit it, and began to puff.

If I was tempted to make a commonplace remark of the beauty of the experience, I did not even have an opportunity to yield to it. I heard the distinct crack of a rifle somewhere back up the hill, followed a split second later by an explosion of bark from the beech tree as a bullet struck it.

There are some drills a man who has served under fire never forgets. I grabbed Holmes's arm and threw him to the ground on the far side of the wall, landing partially on top of him.

"He's trying to kill you!" I shouted. "Stay down!"

I wiggled my body off of my friend's and looked to see if there was any route of escape that would not expose us. There was none.

"Stay here," I ordered Holmes. "I'll see if there is a way around the end of the wall. Don't move."

"My pipe," said Holmes.

"What about your pipe?"

"When you hauled me down, I dropped it, but I think it is on top of the wall. I'll take a look."

He started to stand up and brought his eyes up to the top of the wall, quickly reached across and retrieved his pipe. As he did so, the sharp crack of another rifle shot split the air, followed immediately by an explosion of brick fragments as the bullet hit the face of the brick wall, just inches from Holmes's head.

"HOLMES!" I screamed and tackled him around the waist, pulling him down to the rough ground on our side of the wall. "Are you mad!? He is trying to kill you! STAY DOWN!"

He adjusted his position until he had his back against the wall, and his long legs stretched out in front of him. Then he calmly re-lit his pipe and started to chuckle.

"Have you lost your mind, Holmes? There is nothing funny about someone trying to kill you. That must be Sterndale up there, and he is trying to get rid of you just like he did Tregennis and Sydenham."

"Is he? I think not. Tell me, my dear Doctor, how many times can a lion hunter shoot at a lion and miss before he becomes lunch?"

"What are you talking about?"

"If he had wanted to kill me, he would have. I was a sitting duck up on the wall, and he hit the tree a yard to my left. I put my head above the wall, and he hit a brick a foot below me. He is not trying to kill me, only scare us away. Now, does that not make more sense?"

"Yes, it makes sense, and if you're wrong, you won't have to think about it much longer."

"Ah, but I am sure I am right, and I shall go and have a chat with him and ask what he thinks he is going to accomplish by shooting and deliberately missing me."

He pulled his legs up under his body and sprang to his feet, all energy in an instant. Another shot cracked across the lawn, and it must have sped on past him and ended up somewhere out in the ocean.

Placing his hand on top of the wall, he gave a hop and dexterously lifted his body, planted his posterior on top of the wall, rotated around, and pushed off the far side. A fourth shot hit the wall beside him and then a fifth. He started walking quickly toward the copse of trees in which the shooter must have been concealed. One final shot went off, and then the firing stopped as Holmes came closer and closer to the trees. I shrugged, hopped over the wall, and followed him, taking care to keep the trees, his body, and mine in as close to a straight line as I could.

As soon as he reached the place where the shooter had been standing, he pulled out his glass and began to examine the ground. I joined him and started to look at the small path that led back out of the tress to a hard-surfaced walkway on the other side. It was to no avail.

"He has cleverly walked only on hard surfaces," said Holmes. "I cannot see a print or telltale mark on anything anywhere."

"But why would Sterndale want to do that?" I asked.

"An excellent question, my dear Doctor. A reasonable hypothesis would be that he knows something that he does not want us to know and hopes to frighten us away before we find out."

"Like what?"

"I don't know, and we are on our way back now to the town anyway, so we are not likely to ever know. Come now. Our livery driver's fare keeps moving up with each passing minute."

Chapter Twenty-Five

Let's Eat Indian

We met up with Millie at the manor house, and all three of us climbed into the livery carriage.

"We should," I said, "be back in Penzance in time to have dinner at the hotel."

"Oh, we don't need to do that," said Millie. "We can stay in the little inn in Marazion. It is so much nicer and not much farther along the coast from here. You will enjoy it so much more."

"An excellent suggestion, Miss," said Holmes. "However, we left our baggage at the station in Penzance and would have to return there to fetch it and then retrace our steps to Marazion. Furthermore, when I made our bookings through Thomas Cook, I also had them reserve rooms at the Union Hotel, and I paid in advance. Therefore, let us be on our way."

"But the little inn is so much nicer. It would be worth it to run into the station and come back here. The view out across Mount's Bay is splendid and, in the morning, when the tide is low, we can walk out the causeway to St. Michael's Mount. I have not done that in years. We could have a small adventure now that we have discovered what I hope will be good news. What do you think, John?'

"It sounds to me—"

"No," said Holmes. "Time is of the essence, and I do not have time for any adventure. I already endured one holiday in this slow, sad corner of England and have no interest in another. Come now, the driver will take us back into town."

Having stopped briefly at the railway station to retrieve our baggage, we proceeded into the town to the Union Hotel. The liveryman helped us carry our bags into the lobby and thanked us for the business and the generous gratuity that Holmes added to his fee. Just as we were about to approach the front desk, Millie put her hand on my forearm and held me back.

"John, I know this is silly of me, but I know the man at the front desk from when I used to live here. I found it embarrassing to have Alex and Bertha stare at my forehead and eye, and I do not want to go through that again. Would you mind terribly bringing my key to me so I don't have to explain one more time?"

"Happy to, my dear," I said. "You wait here, and I get it for you."

Twenty minutes later, after having found our rooms and freshened up, the three of us met in the lobby.

"Mr. Holmes?" said Millie.

"Yes, Miss Smith, what is it this time?"

"The food in the hotel is certainly acceptable but so very English. At least you can let me enjoy a small adventure, and we can walk for five minutes and eat Indian. There is a fine little place just down the road, and it serves delicious lamb tikka masala. It would be so much nicer than eating here, and it is a perfect summer evening to walk there."

"A capital idea," I exclaimed before Holmes could object to whatever additional time such an excursion might require.

Millie led us to a small restaurant that bore the pretentious name of *Taj Mahal*. The food was indeed delectable, but I had reminded myself of the very first night I spent in India many years ago. I vividly recalled thinking *When in India, do as the Indians do* and ordering a full dinner, replete with all the requisite spices. At two o'clock in the morning, I had awakened with an excruciating pain in my stomach and thinking *I am going to die before I make it anywhere close to the battlefield.* Needless to say, I recovered and never made that mistake again.

Holmes ate little, and what he did eat, he ate quickly. He was finished well before Millie or me, and he pushed his chair back and stood up.

"You two enjoy the rest of the evening. I have work to do." Whereupon, he departed, leaving us to linger over *rasmali* and a bottle of wine.

"The walk along the promenade," said Millie, "is divine this time of year. Can we go for a stroll?"

We did just that.

In the morning, the three of us returned to the railway station to board the train back to London. Holmes was even more than usually taciturn and remote and said little or nothing to Millie or me. He again sat alone in a separate cabin and left the two of us to enjoy another six hours together, which we did.

She was talkative and optimistic all the way home, imagining and planning what she would now do to improve and expand the *Cornwall Monthly Review*. I repeatedly cautioned her not to count her chickens before they hatched. She nodded and acknowledged the truth of what I had said and then carried right on with her next idea.

"Do you think England could accept another fortnightly review?" she asked me. "Mind you, I would have to find a few more excellent writers. Any suggestions?"

"Can't think of any off the top of my head," I said.

"I can. I know a jolly good one, and I will ask him, and I will not take *no* for an answer."

"You do? Who?"

"You."

I laughed. "My dear, I have a contract already with the *Strand,* and I have no intention of breaking it."

"Oh, John. You could continue to write about Sherlock Holmes for them. But you have such a sensational imagination that you could write an entirely new and different set of stories for me."

"About what? All I know is what I record when Holmes asks me to come along with him. Other than that, and my medical practice, I have a rather dull life."

"Well then, you shall just have to learn how to write fiction. You can make stories up."

"About what?"

"Have you read all those tales that Haggard spins about *She-Who-Must-Be-Obeyed* and Alan Quatermain?"

"Yes, splendid stories."

"Have you heard about Professor William Rutherford and the newspaper fellow, Ned Malone?"

"Yes, why?"

"I think you are just the man to make up characters based on the two of them and send them off to incredible adventures in Africa or South America. You could have them discover some primitive tribe in the Amazon where they still hunt and are hunted by dinosaurs."

"Dinosaurs? You must be joking. No one would ever read stories like that."

"I assure you, they would."

We chatted on like this until we reached Paddington and disembarked from the train. Holmes joined us and was as abrupt as he had been six hours earlier.

"I shall walk home alone. Watson, it might be wise of you to find a cab and escort Miss Smith back to Bermondsey."

"Why do you say that?" I asked.

"Her life may be in danger. We can talk about it later."

He turned and walked away from me, but I was not at all averse to following his suggestion. I suggested to Millie that we might stop for dinner together along the way, but she demurred.

"John, tomorrow is going to be feverish with activity. All of the parties to the dispute about the estate and their lawyers will start jumping around and trying to best each other. I am going to have my hands full."

"Do you know a solicitor who can represent you?"

"I know *of* several, but they are frightfully expensive, far beyond my means."

I took out a pencil and scribbled a name on a page in my notebook, tore it off, and handed it to her.

"This chap is the best in London. He's in the Inner Temple, and if you use my name, he will be willing to help you. And do not worry about his fees. I will look after them. Now don't argue with me. Just call on him first thing tomorrow and demand that he represent your interests."

"Oh, John, you are such a darling, aren't you. Now drop me off at my door and be on your way before I fall in love with you."

I felt so quietly thrilled that as soon as I returned to Baker Street, I took Pilot for a walk in the park and told him all about my weekend adventures.

By the following afternoon, I was told, the lawyers for the estate of Lady Carrington, for Mr. Clive Clapper, for the estate of Saxon Sydenham, for Dr. Leon Sterndale and Lady Williams, and for Miss Millie Smith were at it hammer and tongs. Somewhat to my surprise, Holmes took no interest in the disputes whatsoever. We passed each other briefly in the front room as he was on his way out.

"They will be fighting in the courts for at least a year," he said. "And frankly, I do not care a fig who comes away with what. There is still a murderer on the loose—possibly two of them—who need to be brought to justice. Give any of those literary snobs my regards should you happen to run into them."

I sent notes off to Millie on Tuesday and again on Wednesday, suggesting a dinner together, but she quite understandably declined. Holmes was nowhere to be seen, and I shared my dinner time with an aging cocker spaniel.

To my surprise and delight, on Thursday, she accepted. By the time I arrived at Simpson's for an early supper, she was already seated at a table and had ordered a bottle of Champagne.

"Well, don't you just look like the cat who swallowed the canary," I said as I sat down. She was, indeed, not only smiling, she was ravishing. The goose egg and the black eye had disappeared, and she was dressed in a rather *avant garde* manner and looking ... irresistible.

"That's because I am dining with a brilliant, handsome gentleman, and I am about to tell him my very good news."

"Do tell."

"The *Review* is mine."

"What?!...What do you mean *mine*? What happened?"

"First a toast," she said. "I have already had one glass, and you are going to join me for my second."

We toasted, and I hastened to add. "And now, my dear, please explain."

"Most of the fighting was over the Carrington properties and investments. That is where all the money is. Clive had no interest in the *Review,* and he agreed not to challenge my claim if I would promise I would give Felicity endless hours of work and keep her out of trouble. Lady Williams already has more money than she needs and was interested primarily in getting back the properties Leon sold to Gwendolyn. Such battle as I had was with Mr. Gorman. He's the lawyer representing the estate of Saxon Sydenham."

"He wanted the contract to sell the *Review* to be recognized?"

"No. He had no idea what it was worth. He wanted the cash from the trust fund that was to be set up to run it. I agreed to give that up if he would hand over the reins to the *Review.*"

"You gave up having the income off of twenty-thousand pounds? How are you going to support yourself?"

"Advertising. Our monthly income has doubled in the past two years and, if managed shrewdly, it will continue to grow. And next year, I shall expand and publish an American edition and sell adverts to Yankees. I shall travel to New York twice a year, and I might even take Dr. John Watson with me. That is if he will promise to write some stunning stories for me."

"Who has all the assets? The subscription lists, the articles and stories you had already edited, the agreements with writers and printers?"

"I do. As soon as Mr. Gorman and I reached an agreement, I hired a man and a cart and drove straight away to Saxon's house and retrieved the steamer trunk into which I had put everything. It was all there, and it is now in my safekeeping."

"Splendid," I said and raised my glass again.

We chatted on over dinner, and she continued to expound on her hopes and plans. She was positively joyful, and her countenance radiated her happy state.

I returned to 221B, feeling profoundly happy. I allowed myself some fleeting thoughts of a future traveling on an ocean liner in the company of a beautiful, brilliant, and much-fêted woman. I bounced a little climbing the stairs to our parlor and entered. Then I stopped and looked into the room.

Seated in the armchairs and on the sofa were Sherlock Holmes, Inspectors Lestrade and Farber, and Mrs. Sheridan. Pilot was lying on the rug in front of the hearth and jumped up to his feet and wagged his tail upon seeing me. The others did not get up, and they were not smiling at me.

Chapter Twenty-Six

When You Eliminate the
Almost Impossible

"Watson, my dear friend," said Holmes, "please join us. The empty chair is for you."

"Good heavens," I said. "You all look so glum one would think your favorite cat just died. Tell me what's going on here, and maybe I can cheer you up."

"We have made," said Holmes, "significant progress on the investigation into Lady Carrington's and Saxon Sydenham's murders."

"Have you? Well, congratulations. Well done there, chaps ... and lady."

That Holmes and the two inspectors would meet over such a matter was to be expected. What made no sense at all to me was the presence of Mrs. Sheridan.

"As you," said Holmes, "have already played such a helpful role, we felt it incumbent upon us to bring you up-to-date on the recent developments of the case."

"I am all attention."

"Excellent. Now, as you know, my dear Doctor, one of the principles of scientific reason I apply when investigating a case is *when you have eliminated the impossible—*"

"Yes, yes, Holmes. Of course, I know that. You have said it a hundred times, and I have put it in many of the accounts of your adventures I have published. Please, just get on with your eliminations."

"Thank you. Yes, I do recall your having recorded it several times. In this case, the principle applies with some modifications. Not all possibilities can be eliminated. Some can only be classed as highly unlikely. But let us begin with the impossible ones. You would agree, would you not, that Reverend Chrisparkle and Lady Williams, having departed from the *soirée* before the deadly bottle of Port appeared, can now be eliminated?"

"Certainly."

"And what about Mr. Thoby MacCarthy?"

"The fat dead man? Wasn't that a stunner, Holmes? We go to call on a nasty fellow only to find he saw the entire thing as a lark and then went and died. No, it is almost impossible that he killed Lady Carrington and utterly impossible that he shot Sydenham, since he was already stuffed into a casket himself. Did you hear if the dining table collapsed?" I chuckled out loud at the thought.

"The table notwithstanding, we shall strike him off the list. Now then, who does that leave?"

"The two men who stood to profit," I said. "You know, *cui bono* and all that. Clive Clapper and Saxon Sydenham."

"Quite so. But did you happen to read the weekend edition of the *Manchester Guardian?*"

"I never read any edition of that newspaper. As far as I am concerned, the editors are a bunch of self-righteous revolutionaries."

"That may well be. I read it out of necessity so that I am kept aware of what causes those scribblers are supporting this year. A short article appeared on Sunday in which it was reported that at a meeting at the Albermarle Club, Mr. Clive Merryweather Clapper announced his decision to use *every farthing*—those were the words reported—he was about to receive from the copious proceeds of the Carrington estate to establish a fund honoring Oscar Wilde—"

"Merciful heavens! He was being truthful about his intentions?"

"It appears he was. Therefore, his motive, the acquiring of great personal wealth, vanishes as a motive."

"He might have been so obsessed with doing something in the name of Oscar Wilde that he was driven to commit murder," I said, knowing that what I had uttered bordering on inane.

"How likely is that?" said Holmes.

"Extremely unlikely."

"I agree."

"Jolly good," I said. "That leaves us, among the guests, with the Ouinon woman and Saxon Sydenham. He must have killed her to gain control of her *Review* and then forged the Agreement. Then Sterndale deduced that Sydenham had murdered his mistress and killed him in revenge. Just like he did to that Mortimer Tregennis chap. All terribly logical. I assume you compared the signature on that document with the ones on the copies of her Will."

"I did. They matched."

"They what?"

"The contract to sell the *Review* to Sydenham was valid. It had been signed a few days earlier but had not yet been announced by the time of the *soirée*. He had no reason to kill her. "

"Good lord. Then Sterndale shot him for no reason. What a horrible, bitter, ironic—,"

"Almost Shakespearian," said Holmes.

"Quite so."

"There is a problem with that conclusion. You will agree the Dr. Leon Sterndale is very easily recognized. He is very well-known in Penzance and around the coast of Mount's Bay."

"I should not be surprised."

"I contacted the station master in Penzance. He knows Sterndale well and says he could pick him out of a crowd a hundred yards away, and he tells me that Sterndale arrived in Penzance at one-thirty on the Friday train from Paddington."

"But … but that would mean…"

"Precisely. At the time when Sydenham was being shot with a hunting rifle, the great white hunter was either on a train to Cornwall or already there."

"That makes no sense, Holmes. If he had no part in killing Sydenham, why would he take shots at us?"

"Did he?"

"Did he what? Have no part in killing Sydenham?"

"No. Did he shoot at us?"

"Of course, he did. You knew it was him, Holmes. You said so. Have you changed your mind?"

"I change my mind when the facts change, my good man. What do you do? I could see that I had been wrong. The same station master told me that Sterndale bought a ticket for and boarded the late afternoon train back to London. It left the station ten minutes after shots were fired at us. He could not possibly have made it back from the manor to the station in that time."

"But … well then …who's left? Only that Ouinon woman. She struck me as crazier than a jaybird, but there must be some hidden animosity, some hatred that we do not know about that would lead her to kill her benefactor."

"Perhaps there is," said Holmes, "and for that reason, we shall pay another visit to her shortly and interrogate her more thoroughly."

"Ah, good to know. And who would ever have suspected her."

"She is not the only remaining suspect," said Holmes.

"But who else is there?"

Here, Inspector Frank Farber spoke up, "Do you believe, sir, that the girl could have poisoned Lady Carrington?"

"The girl? You mean Felicity Clapper?"

"Yes."

"No." Now the conversation had become ridiculous. "Come now. I would not be surprised that she has read and written about more horrible ways to murder someone than any of us could ever imagine. And she may be precocious to the point of being obnoxious, but she had no reason to harm Lady Carrington. And it is beyond belief that she would risk killing Millie. She quite adores her. No, she's out of the question."

"I agree," said Farber.

I was racking my brain and landed on the only remaining possibility.

"It must have been Sterndale," I said. "He is the only one left. You said yourself, Holmes, that he had the ability, the stealth to sneak in past the guests and slip poison onto the bottle. Are you going to bring him in, Inspector?"

"No, Doctor. During the entire time the *soirée* was taking place, he was delivering a gripping, thrilling, heart-stopping talk to the Reform Club on Pall Mall about his latest self-glorifying adventure hunting a ferocious, man-eating lion in darkest Africa. At least that is what was written on the program card, and the club manager confirmed that he was indeed there and gave his lecture and, even if not up to the expectations, he did not depart and spent the night at the club."

"My dear chap," said Holmes, "Our list of suspects is down to two."

Now I was thoroughly confused and started to say, "I don't under…" when a feeling first of shock, then anger and then outrage swept through my entire body and soul, and I exploded.

"HOLMES! What you are implying is absurd! Utterly ridiculous! There is no possibility whatsoever that Mildred Smith could have murdered Gwendolyn Carrington. What has come over you?! I will not stand for such an unforgivable insult to her!"

I was on my feet and shouting at him. I added several more expletives that I have not recorded. I could not remember a time in my life when I had so completely lost my temper at Sherlock Holmes.

As he stood and walked slowly toward me, I involuntarily clenched my fists, and it was all I could do to refrain from smashing my right hand into his face.

"Please, my dear friend," he said, placing his hands on my upper arms. "Sit down and listen. Please."

He was firmly pushing me back to my chair, and I resisted, refusing to back off on inch.

"Get a hold of yourself," he whispered, "and hear us out. That is all I ask."

Chapter Twenty-Seven

I Don't Believe You

Reluctantly, I stepped back and sat down, but my fists were still clenched, and my heart was pounding.

"It's impossible! Mildred Smith almost died herself!" I said.

"Did she?" asked Holmes.

"You were there! You saw and heard what I saw."

"I did, and we both saw and heard very little. And do you recall suggesting I recruit both Miss Smith and Mrs. Sheridan to assist in my investigation?"

"Well, yes, but what does that have to do with Mildred's being poisoned?"

"I followed your advice and asked Mrs. Sheridan to report to me privately on her meetings with the other guests and carry out additional searches as directed. Mrs. Sheridan," said Holmes, now looking at her, "will you kindly inform Dr. Watson of your answer to my question about Miss Smith's condition that day?"

"Dr. Watson," she said, looking directly at me and giving a small bow of respect, "what I will say to you is what I, as a nurse, would report to a doctor. Kindly accept what I say in that regard. You and I are both familiar with the effects that a serious but non-fatal ingesting of a poison like cyanide has on the body. The patient will vomit violently to expel the substance, but for the next forty-eight hours, will experience severe headaches, palpitations of the heart, and disorders of the digestive tract, including diarrhea. Is that correct?"

I nodded.

"Miss Smith had none," she said. "A few minutes after you and the police had departed, she got up out of bed and carried on as if nothing adverse had happened to her."

"Good heavens," I said. "That only proves that she has a strong constitution and ingested only a small amount. Besides, Mildred Smith had no reason at all to want to do away with Lady Carrington."

"Are you sure?" said Holmes. "We were informed that Saxon Sydenham had paid previous visits to the house and had been negotiating the purchase of the *Review*. Would such a move by Carrington not have been a vile betrayal of her promise to Miss Smith that she would be given the right to the publication that she had so diligently and brilliantly established?"

"And why shouldn't she be angry? And now I suppose you are going to accuse her of shooting Saxon Sydenham when she learned that it had, in fact, been sold."

"Is it possible that after learning of that from you, she might wish to stop the sale by getting rid of Sydenham?"

"Holmes! You…you looked at the place where the shooter had stood. You said the footprints were from a large man. Those were your words! Millie is not a large man. Your conjectures are…they are nonsense!"

"What I said was that it was a large man, *walking slowly*. I said that because the length of the stride was strange for a man as tall as Sterndale. It was not, however, the wrong length for a shorter woman who may have donned a large man's boots to disguise her identity."

"Holmes!" I said, getting more and more exasperated. "That is lunacy! She was not a marksman, and where did the gun come from?"

"Mrs. Sheridan reported that Dr. Sterndale had placed a Winchester hunting rifle in his closet in his bedroom in the Carrington house for convenience sake. As to her ability to shoot it, you did tell me, did you not, that her father had taught her to hunt and fish? Given her drive to excel at everything she undertook, I expect that she is a superb marksman."

"Impossible! She was out cold when Sydenham was shot. He had beaten her and knocked her out with chloroform before hauling away the steamer trunk."

"Had he? Are you sure? Mrs. Sheridan, could you speak to that, please."

The woman again gave a respectful nod to me before speaking. "Doctor Watson, sir, as you will know, every nurse over time becomes something of a martinet for making sure that all surfaces are always wiped clean and that there is a place for everything and everything goes back in its place. I extended that discipline to my management of Lady Carrington's house."

"I am sure you did. What has that to do with Sydenham's attack on her and his taking away the assets of the *Review*?"

"Sir, when I inspected the kitchen on my rounds before supper, I noticed that one of the paring knives and one of the tea towels were not in the place they had been left. The cooks and the maid would not dare leave them like that. And there was a smudge of facial cosmetic on the door frame."

"For pity sake woman! You cannot be seriously suggesting that she inflicted the beating on herself."

"I am only reporting what I observed, Doctor. You might also wish to know that the steamer trunk never left the house. Someone had slid it down the stairs and into a far corner of the basement."

"Sydenham could have done that himself. It could have been inconvenient for him to take it away then, and he could have planned to return for it."

"Are you sure," asked Holmes, "that Sydenham was ever in the house?"

"Of course, he was. You found his handkerchief. It was full of chloroform and his cologne."

"Ah yes, the handkerchief. I did indeed find one that had been carelessly tossed aside. And Mr. Saxon Sydenham was indeed fond of cologne. The brand he used was *4711,* and he used it so heavily that he might as well have tattooed the numbers on his hip to remind him of the only type he ever used. The scent on the handkerchief, however, was not *4711*. It was the original *Eau de Cologne* by Farina. And being a man as fastidious about his appearance and costume as Beau Brummell, Mr. Sydenham would never toss his handkerchief aside and leave the house without it. The handkerchief was not his."

"You are implying that she put it there, aren't you? Well, it could have been anybody's. Everything you have said so far does nothing to prove that Mildred Smith did anything amiss. And, frankly, I am finding this conversation tedious and annoying. So, if you have nothing else to say, you will kindly excuse me. I have other matters to attend to."

"There is," said Holmes, "one other item."

"Then out with it and get this nonsense over with."

"It concerns our time in Cornwall. When do you suppose Miss Smith was there previously?"

"That is a ridiculous question. I have absolutely no idea. The staff at the manor said they had not seen her for a long time. Beyond that, I don't know, and neither do you."

"Did you not think it strange that she wanted to stay at another hotel, and that when we arrived at the one in town, she avoided being seen by the staff at the desk or in the dining room?"

"Not at all. She told us why, and they were perfectly good reasons."

"Not good enough for me," he said. "I regarded them as unconvincing and inadequate. So, during the night, I left my room and made my way to the front desk. It was vacant at that hour, but I examined the register. Miss Mildred Smith had stayed there just two weeks ago."

"But why would she do that? Maybe it was another Mildred Smith," I said, knowing that it was not.

"Because she secretly visited the manor and added the final footnote, the *codicil,* to the Will."

"Inconceivable! It was locked up in the safe. We were with her. She did not know it was there, and she certainly did not know the combination."

"I suspect she knew both."

"And do you also suspect that it was she who shot at us? That is absurd if you do."

"I do so suspect. There was a gun room in the house, and she may have been trying to force us to direct the investigation to Dr. Sterndale, who, quite inconsiderately, was no longer around to shoot at us. And one more item. I have already told you that the signatures on the contract with Sydenham matched the signature on the main portion of the Will. The signature on the final codicil was close to a match, but not convincing. I had the documents submitted to an expert analyst, and I expect he will report that the one on the codicil was forged. However, the handwriting used for the codicil itself was unmistakable. I recognized it. It belonged to Miss Smith."

"How could you possibly know that? You have never seen anything she has written."

"The name and address on the first note she sent you, and the later note telling you about her having been beaten were the same."

I was back on my feet and pacing the length of the room. Pilot had hopped up and was dogging my footsteps, almost causing me to trip over him. My mind and my stomach were in turmoil, and I snapped at Holmes.

"I do not accept any part of your imagined accusation. But I demand to know what you are going to do next to her. Are you going to charge her with murder?"

Inspector Lestrade answered me. "No, Doctor, we are not. Tomorrow morning, we will pay her a respectful visit and request that she come with us to Scotland Yard and answer some questions. Our interrogation will, I will fully admit, be quite intense."

"Then I am coming with you. As her personal physician, I have the right to accompany her."

"No, Doctor Watson," said Lestrade. "You do not, and you cannot. I assure you, sir, that having known you for over twenty years, I have nothing but the highest respect for your character and integrity. It is because of that, as a courtesy to you that your friend Sherlock Holmes insisted, and I agreed, that we were obligated to inform you of our evidence and our plans. Miss Smith will be informed of her rights and will have thetitill opportunity to request the presence of a solicitor should she so desire. However, this is now a matter for the police, and we will proceed in accordance with established regulations."

Lestrade stood up, and Inspector Farber and Mrs. Sheridan did likewise.

"Good evening, gentlemen," Lestrade said to me and Holmes. "It is time for us to be on our way."

They departed, leaving me to glare at Holmes. I was livid.

"Holmes," I began.

"Please, Watson, my friend, I am really very sorry. From the depths of my heart, let me say that I have wished to Heaven that this case would not unfold the way it has. If I could have done anything to have it turn out differently, I would. All I can ask of you, all I beg from you, is that you let the wheels of justice run their course. It is now out of my hands, just as it is out of yours. I will promise you that tomorrow morning, as soon as the interview has taken place in Scotland Yard, I will return here and apprise you of what happened. You may take whatever action you deem appropriate after that, but until then, you have to let the laws of England be followed."

Had I tried to say anything, I might have screamed at him and said things I would later regret. So, I said nothing. I turned and ascended the stairs to my bedroom.

I paced back and forth in my small room, alternately lying down on the bed and getting back up again and pacing some more. Reading a novel did not help. I could not concentrate on more than a few sentences without having my mind overwhelmed with anger and the terrifying flicker of doubt that Holmes might be right.

At eleven o'clock, I was still wide awake, and I heard Holmes retreat to his bedroom. By that time, I was on my bed but still fully dressed. I lay there, turning from one side to another and mostly staring, wide-eyed, at the darkness above me. Somehow, from somewhere, just after midnight, a thought came into my mind. The thought became a plan, and I rose from my bed and slipped off my shoes. In complete darkness and silence, I descended the stairs to our front room. As I crossed the floor in my stocking feet, shoes in hands, I heard the unmistakable sound of an old dog moving toward me and panting heavily.

Then I felt something bumping into my shins. I knelt down and rubbed Pilot's head.

"Not a sound, old boy, not a sound. I will not be gone long."

Taking one step very slowly after the other until all seventeen were behind me, I crept down the stairs to our front door. Looking back up, I could see the dark outline of the shadow of a dog's head, lying on its paws, and looking at me.

Ever so carefully, I opened our front door, stepped out, closed it silently behind me, pulled my shoes back on, and started walking quickly south on Baker Street.

Chapter Twenty-Eight

What Happened After Midnight

In the hour after midnight, the streets of London are empty and quiet. There were no cabs on Baker Street, and I hurried to Marylebone, where I knew I could always find one at the railway station. I hopped up into the first I saw and gave the driver an address in Bermondsey.

There was at least one thing I could do for her, and I did not think it could be called an obstruction of justice.

The cab rolled along quickly, meeting not a single delay. From Marylebone all the way along Oxford, down Regent and on to the Thames, we passed no more than six cabs and a few uniformed constables walking their nighttime beat. Once across Blackfriar's Bridge and into the south shore, we passed several clusters of Southwark revelers staggering out of the taverns and singing loudly and far off-key.

At a few minutes before one o'clock, I tapped with my fingernail on the door of the small house where Millie Smith lived. There was no response, and I tapped again, several times, each round somewhat harder than the last until I heard movement on the other side.

"Who is it!? What do you want?" a voice called from behind the door.

"Millie. It's me, John. I have to talk to you."

The door opened.

"John?! What in the world are you—,"

"I'll explain," I said as I gently pushed the door back and entered the house.

The lamps were low, but I could see that she was clad in nothing more than a thin summer nightgown and an open house coat and had let her hair fall loosely over her shoulders and down her back. I took her hand and led her into the small front parlor.

"Millie, please sit down and listen. Your life may depend on it."

She sat down, and I quickly explained that Holmes and Lestrade would be coming for her in the morning. I did not go into detail about their suspicions, but I scribbled out the name and address of one of the finest firms of solicitors in London who specialized in criminal defense.

I handed it to her. "Tomorrow morning, get up very early and get out of here. Go to the door of this firm, wait until they open it, and get inside. Tell them you need the best man they have and are willing to pay any fee. I will cover the cost. Do not answer any questions, whether in his office or at Scotland Yard, without your lawyer beside you. Do you understand? You have to do this."

I could see her nodding her head in the near darkness. "But why, John? Why are they doing this?"

I began to repeat the so-called evidence but had uttered no more than a few sentences when she stood up, walked across the small room, and sat down in my lap. She put her arms around my neck and lowered her head to my shoulder.

"There is no need to tell me," she said. "That's what lawyers are paid to listen to. I have a better idea."

With that, she pressed her lips to mine and kissed me passionately. And then the kisses became feverish. I could feel the heat of her body through the thin cotton of her nightgown.

For the sake of decorum and reticence, I shall not describe the events of the next hour except to say that I had not experienced such fiery joy since the days of my honeymoon with Mary Morstan many years ago.

By three o'clock, I was back in the darkness of Baker Street but feeling an overwhelming sense of satisfaction with myself for having provided the best form of protection I could for her, and, at the same time, thoroughly euphoric. I approached 221B in silence, took off my shoes, turned the key slowly in the lock, opened the door, and slipped inside. In the darkness, I saw a shadow move at the top of the stairs, and for a moment, I froze. Then I heard the familiar panting and identified the form of a spaniel, now standing up and waiting for me. Once at the top of the stairs, I bent down and ruffled his head and scratched behind his ear.

"All right, old boy. Back to bed for both of us."

He wagged his backend and watched me until I climbed the stairs back up to my bedroom.

In my bedroom, again in silence and darkness, I changed into my nightclothes and lay down on the bed. For a few short minutes, I felt the peace and well-being that come, I am told, with an overwhelming sense of loving and being loved.

Then I fell fast asleep.

I must have slept soundly as it was well after seven when I awoke. I bathed and dressed quickly and descended to find, as I had expected, Holmes's having already departed for the day. The breakfast table still held a selection of pastries, boiled eggs, cheese, and a carafe of now-lukewarm coffee. I gave my morning greetings to Pilot and, being slightly hungry, tucked into a pleasant repast and turned to chat with the spaniel.

"What do you say, old boy? It's a marvelous spring morning. How about a stroll in the park?"

I found his leash, and we both descended the stairs, he somewhat slowly and cautiously. Older dogs are not as confident as puppies and make sure that they have securely landed on the step below them before continuing to the next. But he was soon down, and we passed at least two hours strolling through the Regent's Park on a perfect summer morning. We watched as mothers and nannies played with their children, and some adventurous boys sailed their homemade boats in the Boating Lake.

I had mentally calculated the time until Holmes's return. I knew that he would have to stop and pick up Lestrade on the Embankment and that the good inspector never crossed the threshold of his office before eight. From there, it was a half-hour in morning traffic to Bermondsey, and from there another half-hour to Gray's Inn where the offices of Bickers, Argue and Phibbs were located. Only then could they begin their questioning and, lawyers being lawyers and charging by the minute, the interview could drag on for two hours or more. It would be at almost noon before Holmes returned.

Noon came and went, as did one o'clock. I redeemed the time by writing up my account of a recent case and reading a novel I had purchased at one of the many small bookstores off Charing Cross Road.

At half-past one, I spoke again to my canine friend. "It is altogether too nice a day to spend inside, old boy. How about another walk? Just a short one, though. No more than half-an-hour. He agreed, and off we went.

On returning, I was met with a shout from Mrs. Hudson.

"There's a letter came for you. Couriered by a bicycle-boy. It's waiting for you on the coffee table."

The two of us ascended the stairs, neither moving as adroitly as we might have a few years ago, and entered the front room. Pilot sauntered over to his domain on the rug by the hearth, and I sat down in front of the coffee table and reached for the package.

It was a calendar-sized envelope that had a distinct bulge in the middle. It bore my name and address in a handwriting that I recognized immediately. I opened it and extracted a letter and a small, hard object wrapped in a portion of a silk scarf. My curiosity aroused, I unwound the scarf and out fell a note and a very large ring with a gleaming amethyst surrounded by an unusually high mound of diamonds.

I unfolded the note and read:

When, by fate, our paths crossed again less than two short weeks ago, I was wearing this ring. I want you to keep it as a memento of our all too brief time together. It is my hope that when you look at it, you will remember only the hours of joy and passion we shared and nothing else. With all my love, Millie.

I was beyond perplexed. I looked at the ring and, not wanting to leave it out lest Pilot find it amusing, slipped it into my pocket and opened the letter. It was neatly typed, and I started to read it. With each line, my hands began to tremble until I was beside myself. It ran:

My dearest John:

   I do not expect you to ever understand what I have done, but please know this: Lady Gwendolyn Ottoline Carrington was a vile, wicked woman who used and abused people as if they were expendable toys. She did not deserve to live.

   Twenty years ago, she hired me as the editor of the Review with the explicit promise that should I build it into a successful literary journal, she would turn over the ownership to me when she retired or lost her interest in it. Two months ago, we passed that milestone as I did what was needed to develop it into the most respected journal of its kind in England and to increase the income until it was self-sufficient. When I approached her a month ago about her promise, she replied by saying, "Ta ta, dearie. I've changed my mind. I am going to sell it to that Saxon fellow. Maybe you can work for him."

I cannot begin to express the rage I felt toward her. It was not hers to sell. It was mine. She had done nothing except use the undeserved wealth she had acquired by a fortunate marriage and widowhood to pay a few bills. I alone had spent the endless hours managing the business affairs and holding the hands of talented but childish authors and turning their rough work into masterpieces.

Thus, I put a plan into place, one that I knew was more diabolically clever than the most conniving I had read in all those murder mysteries. It almost worked.

I had to amend it when you told me that the sale to Sydenham had indeed been signed. Then I had no choice but to remove him. My only mistake, and it was indeed nearly fatal to me, was to imagine I could be smarter than Sherlock Holmes.

Fortunately, you, my dear friend and lover, came to my rescue just in time. My plan to flee England had been at the ready in case I needed it, and as soon as you departed my home in the small hours of this morning, I put it into action. I have escaped. I have fled to the Cape Province, or to New York, or to Buenos Aires, or to Sydney, or to whichever remote city you can name. It is sad that I shall never see you again, but some things cannot be avoided. You will always have my heart, but my Review owns my mind and my soul.

I remain, yours and yours alone, Millie

P.S. Kindly advise Sherlock Holmes not to attempt to find me. He will put another innocent young life at risk if he tries.

"Dear God in heaven, NOOO!!" I screamed as I repeatedly smashed my fists down on the coffee table. My doing so had the unwelcome result of startling the dog, who barked loudly, and disturbing Mrs. Hudson, who hollered up the stairs to ask if I was in pain. I shouted back that I was fine. It was nothing.

It was not nothing. It was catastrophic. How could I? How could I have been such a fool?

In a fit of rage, I crumpled up the letter and was about to throw it, uselessly, into the unlit hearth. My common sense prevailed, and I knew that I risked destroying evidence in a case of murder. I sat back down, put my elbows to my knees, dropped my face into my hands, and sobbed.

I was frozen in that place, sobbing, until I felt the distinct sensation of a dog's tongue licking the backs of my hands. I looked down at him, and he looked up at me. Then he scampered across the room and fetched his leash with his teeth and brought it to me. His instructions were clear.

"All right, old boy, maybe that's the best thing we can do."

I uncrumpled the letter and laid it out on the table so that Holmes would see it when he returned, and then, for the next two hours, Pilot and I strolled aimlessly through the park. Several times, I felt I could not go on and dropped my body onto a bench and let my chin fall down on my chest. Pilot waited patiently at my feet for about ten minutes on each occasion before barking at me and demanding that I get up and keep walking. It was four o'clock by the time we returned to 221B.

Holmes had still not returned, so I poured myself a large glass of brandy and attempted to drown my sorrows. It was a stupid thing to do. By five o'clock, I was no less devastated but much more muddle-brained. I opened our bay window and stood beside it, hoping the fresh air would clear my head. As I looked out, a police wagon with the familiar markings of Scotland Yard stopped in front of our door. Sherlock Holmes stepped out.

Chapter Twenty-Nine

I Would Like to Die

His steps as he climbed the stairs were slow. Upon entering the room, he put down his hat and stick, and only then did he look up and see me standing across the room. For what seemed an eternity, he looked at me, a sadness in his eyes that I had never seen before. I looked back at him and then nodded toward to coffee table where the letter lay open. He picked it up, sat down in his chair, and read it.

Finally, he looked up at me. "My friend, she also convinced me. She had a motive in misleading us and she played her part brilliantly."

"But you saw through her. I was played for a fool until the end."

"The only difference is that you were blinded by the dangerous mixture of romantic emotions and your animal spirits. They are a deadly combination. Now come, sit down. We have some ground to cover."

I sat across from him and offered a comment. "Might I assume that she was not at the office of the law firm?"

"Correct. The note telling us to find her there was posted on her door, but when we reached Gray's Inn and the lawyers' offices, they said they had never heard of her. We immediately dashed off around London to all of the major train stations and sent messages to every port of call and every passenger shipping line in the country. She vanished and covered her tracks. We could not find a trace of her."

"Did you search Lady Carrington's home? Was the steamer trunk still there."

"We did, and it was gone. She took her precious *Review* with her."

After that, we fell into another brief time of silence. It ended when he asked me a question.

"Do you have the ring?"

I was startled. "Yes, I do," and I retrieved it from my pocket and put in on the table. "How did you know about it?"

He picked it up and looked at it closely, then took out his glass and examined it from every angle. A flash of a smile appeared and faded and, holding the ring by the shank, twisted the entire setting. It turned, and he kept twisting another half turn until it became detached. Beneath the amethyst and diamonds, it looked as if there was a small hollow cup, about the size of half a thimble.

"*Voila,*" he said. "The murder weapon. You can put more than enough cyanide in here to kill anyone when you drop it into a glass of Port."

"But how did you know?"

"It is said that Lucrezia Borgia had such a ring and used it to do away with unwanted husbands and lovers. Lady Williams made reference to it in the eighth chapter of her lurid biography."

"And Saxon Sydenham?"

"In last January's edition of the *Review,* the murder mystery told how the killer had waited until a ship's whistle blasted before firing a bullet into a parlor. The victim jumped up and looked at the damage to his wall and was subsequently shot dead. Does that sound familiar?"

Again, we lapsed into silence before I had to satisfy my curiosity.

"How did you know? When did you begin to suspect her?"

"That, my friend, was your doing."

"It was? How?"

"You said that, long ago, some conflict had come between you. I assumed that it must have been a significant matter of principle to cause the ending of what promised to be a compelling romantic friendship. And I knew that if Doctor John Watson acted on a matter of principle, it could only mean that he was in the right and the other party in the wrong. Was my deduction correct? What happened? I suspect you have not, in truth, forgotten."

"No," I sighed, "I have not. There was another young editor at *Beeton's,* a sweet-natured young fellow named Ambrose Moss. He was only twenty years old and had already graduated from Oxford and he was…I would have to say that he was a genius and the most brilliant master of the English language I had ever met…to this day. He was Lady Carrington's first choice as the editor of her new journal."

"And did Miss Mildred torpedo that choice?"

"She did. Millie wanted the position. She could see that it was her ticket to achieve her dreams. So, she spread false gossip about the lad and told a few well-chosen people that Ambrose was secretly a member of some radical anarchist political society who wanted to confiscate all land owned by titled nobility and re-distribute it to the peasant farmers. As Lady Carrington was one such landowner, she was having none of that and dropped him and hired Millie."

"And you found out and were not pleased?"

"I did, and we had words…harsh words…and soon after that, she moved off to Cornwall, and I did not pursue her."

"And young Mr. Moss? What happened to him?"

"He moved to America and, last I heard, had secured a position at the University of Iowa teaching farm boys how to write sentences and paragraphs."

Holmes took out his pipe, lit it and slowly inhaled and exhaled.

"Somewhere in the Good Book it asks if a leopard can change its spots, does it not?"

"It does, and she didn't."

We lapsed again into silence before I asked him what his plans were now.

"I shall send notices to police forces throughout the country and around the world. I can make a thousand mistakes whilst searching for a killer, but he, or she, can only make one. It may not be this year, or next, or the year after, but eventually, I will find her."

He puffed again on his pipe and then turned to me.

"And what, my friend, do you plan to do?"

"I would like to die."

"That is not allowed."

"Why not? I deserve to after what I have done."

"Because then I would be left to look after your mangy old spaniel and I'd rather not."

We ate our supper in silence, and afterward, I attempted to write and then to read and failed at both. I moved my chair so I could look out the front window, folded my arms across my chest, and stared into the twilight.

I sat there, paralyzed with humiliation for at least an hour. The dark time of my soul was interrupted by a knock on the Baker Street door. Mrs. Hudson attended to it, and I heard a man's steps rapidly climbing up to our floor. Clive Clapper burst into the room.

"Holmes, I need your help," he said. His face was flushed, and he was sweating heavily. "I can't find her."

"Find who?" said Holmes.

"Felicity. My daughter. She's gone."

I could hear Holmes mutter a quiet, "Oh no," before he asked our visitor to sit down.

"What happened?" he asked.

"She has not come home. She is always home for supper. I insist on it."

"Go on."

"I was out last night. Somewhat late."

"Late, or until well into this morning?"

"Until about nine this morning. The maid said Mildred Smith had come by around seven and had offered to take her with her for the day. I thought nothing of it. Felicity adores her. They've spent many days together. When she had not come home for supper, I was annoyed and walked over to Mildred's home to fetch her. There were several policemen clustered around the door. They said they had no idea where Miss Smith was. So, I ran over to Lady Carrington's house on the chance they were there. But there was another constable standing guard at that door. He gave me the same answer. He was a decent chap, and he could see that I was upset and asked me what had happened. I told him, and he looked alarmed and said that the best advice he could give me was to go and see Sherlock Holmes immediately."

"And have you come here directly?"

"No, I thought he must be talking nonsense. These coppers have far too sensational imaginations. I ran back to my house and into her bedroom. Many of her clothes were missing, and there was a note on her dresser."

He handed it to Holmes, who then passed it over to me. In a girl's handwriting, it read:

Dear Daddy: Don't worry about me. I promise to write. Felicity

"And then," said Clapper, "I rushed over here. What is going on? Do you know? Tell me."

"Ah, well, at least she appears to have left willingly and was not kidnapped," said Holmes.

"She's still gone. Look, I may not be the finest moral example to a fifteen-year-daughter, and frankly, she can be an annoying little prig, and most of the time I do not like her much, and she feels the same way about me. But I am still her father. I am responsible for her. Is she in danger? Tell me!"

Holmes got up, walked over to the mantel and poured a snifter of brandy for Clive Clapper. After giving it to him, he sat down and concisely related to him the significant details of the case, letting Clapper know that Mildred Smith was now being sought for the murders of both Lady Carrington and Mr. Sydenham.

"Good gaaawd," he exclaimed. "The woman is a monster. Would she hurt Felicity? I wouldn't think so. They were friends. Felicity loved working with her."

Holmes took out the letter I had received from Millie.

"The contents of this letter are confidential evidence in our investigation," he said, "but you should be made aware of the postscript."

He read the now-horrifying words, *"Kindly advise Sherlock Holmes not to attempt to find me. He will put another innocent young life at risk if he tries."*

Clapper's face lost all its color, and he gasped, "That woman is the devil."

Chapter Thirty

What is Tatamagouche?

wo years passed since the events I have recorded above. During that time, Mr. Clive Clapper received a letter every fortnight from his daughter. One was postmarked New York, the next San Francisco, the next Madrid, and the next Auckland, and so on from cities all over the globe. Clapper turned every one of them over to Holmes as soon as it was received and read. The contents were chatty and assured him that she was safe and in good health, but gave no clue as to her location.

"She is using an international mail forwarding service that has offices around the world," said Holmes. "It is a common practice of criminals who wish to disguise their whereabouts. There is no way of tracking the letter back to the sender."

To my relief, after my colossal blunder, Holmes continued to ask for my help with many of his cases. However, none of them concerned any unmarried, attractive woman beyond the age of thirty.

I carried on my life as a widower and made myself content with my work, my writing, my assistance to Holmes, and my daily walks and conversations with Pilot. Every day during the spring, summer, and fall, we would walk over to the park. Come winter, I carried him down the stairs—he was too old to manage them by himself—and we took a cab over to some of the shopping arcades and quiet streets that housed a selection of interesting shops. My favorite was Cecil Street, just beyond Charing Cross Road, where the best used-book stores were clustered. I would leave Pilot tied to a lamppost while I perused some of the treasures inside.

It was on just such an occasion that I was in one of my customary haunts when I picked up copies of a Dickens novel I had never read, a volume of somewhat risqué verse by Charles Baudelaire—in translation—and then a slender blue book caught my eye. The title read *The Tatamagouche Fortnightly Review: a collection of the finest current literary offerings from New England and Atlantic Canada.* I had never heard of it, but as the price for the used edition was only sixpence, I added it to my basket.

As soon as we were back in 221B, I opened my latest find and started to read the first story. It had the catchy title of *The Adventure of the Single Tycoon* by some writer named James Matson. The clever first sentence ran:

The Ernest Appleton Gardner, Esquire marriage, and its curious termination, have long ceased to be a subject of interest in those exalted circles in which the unfortunate bridegroom moves.

A clever way to start a story, I mused to myself. Rather like one I remembered writing. I read on until I came to a sentence a few lines further down. It ran:

As I have reason to believe, however, that the full facts have never been revealed to the general public, and as my friend Octavius Fox had a considerable share in clearing the matter up, I feel that no memoir of him would be complete without some little sketch of this remarkable episode.

My eyes widened, and I kept reading.

"The gall!" I cried out to myself. "This is *my* story! Some miserable scribbler over there in the colonies has pirated my story, changed the names, and passed it off as his own."

I flipped the pages to see if anything else I had written had been stolen and copied. There was nothing else. I did see a poem entitled *Porphyria's Second Lover* and read it quickly. It was a somewhat titillating account in a similar poetic style to Robert Browning of a woman who invited a handsome stranger into her home, engaged in passionate activity, and then strangled him by his necktie. Brilliantly written, I thought. There may be some original talent off in the far corners of the New World after all.

In the middle of the journal was a story by a Mr. Alexander MacDonald, the Keppoch Bard of Nova Scotia. It was presented on one page in Gaelic and on the facing page in English.

The next entry was a chapter of a biography of Lucrezia Borgia, and it was followed by an intriguing murder mystery, and an insightful critique of a novel that had appeared a few years back. I was partway through reading it when a distinct chill came over me, and I became aware of what it was I had stumbled upon. I quickly turned the pages back to the title page, where the name of Martha Jones (Miss) was given as the editor. The copyright page claimed that it was printed in a town by the odd-sounding name that appeared on the cover and was available only by limited subscription or from better bookstores in New England and Atlantic Canada.

I put the book down on the coffee table and looked over at my now very old friend.

"We found her, Pilot, old boy. We found her."

He looked up at me and twitched his ear.

"Now, what am I going to do?" I asked him. "If I give this to Holmes, he'll find a way to rescue the girl, have Millie arrested and brought back to England…and they'll hang her."

I was soon back up on my feet and pacing the length of the room one more time. Holmes's words about the inevitable conflict between affairs of the heart and the singular pursuit of justice echoed in the recesses of my brain. On my third traverse of the room, I looked over at the door to the staircase. Pilot was sitting there, his leash in his mouth.

Before picking him up and taking him down the stairs, I took a piece of paper and wrote a note to Holmes. I slipped it into the pages of *The Tatamagouche Fortnightly Review* with part of it protruding so it could not be missed, and I left the volume on the table where Holmes would sit for his next meal. Then I carried my old friend down the steps, and we took ourselves on one more walk.

My note read: *My dear Holmes: You had better take a look at this. Your friend, John Watson.*

A request to all readers:

After reading this story, please help the author and future readers by taking a moment to write a short, constructive review on the site from which you purchased the book. Thank you.   CSC

Dear Sherlockian Reader:

The Bermondsey Set is modeled on The Bloomsbury Group, an informal network of an influential group of artists, art critics, writers and an economist, many of whom lived in the West Central 1 district of London known as Bloomsbury. They emerged a few years following the date of this story and so could not be used directly. However, their influence has extended to this day and they are fun to read and learn about.

St. James, Bermondsey is still the Anglican parish church in the Bermondsey community of London. The Mayflower pub was in operation on the south bank of the Thames in 1903 and still is.

Simpson's-in-the-Strand was one of Sherlock Holmes's favorite restaurants. It is still in operation and serves a fabulous roast-beef-on-a-trolley. The Taj Mahal Indian restaurant was not in Penzance in 1903 but is there today, so I borrowed it.

The properties of the Duchy of Cornwall were owned then and still are by the Prince of Wales. They are the source of much of his wealth and that of his offspring. For many centuries, Cornwall was the source of tin for much of the western world. Today, not so much.

The truth about Lucrezia Borgia is lost in the mists of history. The rumors and legends of her beauty, her habits of poisoning unwanted husbands and lovers, and her use of a large ring as a murder weapon live on.

Tatamagouche is a lovely small town in Nova Scotia. The idea of a *Tatamagouche Review* came from the now-extinct *Tamarack Review,* a superb Canadian literary journal that published regularly from 1956 until 1982 and which I remember reading when I was an English major at the University of Toronto.

There are many 'Easter Eggs' inserted in the story. Hope you have fun spotting them.

Pilot was the name of Mr. Rochester's dog. Reader: Pilot did not bark.

Happy sleuthing and deducing, Craig

About the Author

In May of 2014 the Sherlock Holmes Society of Canada – better known as The Bootmakers – announced a contest for a new Sherlock Holmes story. Although he had no experience writing fiction, the author submitted a short Sherlock Holmes mystery and was blessed to be declared one of the winners. Thus inspired, he has continued to write new Sherlock Holmes Mysteries since and is on a mission to write a new story as a tribute to each of the sixty stories in the original Canon. He has been writing these stories while living in Toronto, the Okanagan, Buenos Aires, Bahrain and Manhattan. Several readers of New Sherlock Holmes Mysteries have kindly sent him suggestions for future stories. You are welcome to do likewise at craigstephencopland@gmail.com.

More Historical Mysteries
by Craig Stephen Copland

www.SherlockHolmesMystery.com

Open website to look inside and download

Studying Scarlet. Starlet O'Halloran, a fabulous mature woman, who reminds the reader of Scarlet O'Hara (but who, for copyright reasons cannot actually be her) has arrived in London looking for her long-lost husband, Brett (who resembles Rhett Butler, but who, for copyright reasons, cannot actually be him). She enlists the help of Sherlock Holmes. This is an unauthorized parody, inspired by Arthur Conan Doyle's *A Study in Scarlet* and Margaret Mitchell's *Gone with the Wind.*

The Sign of the Third. Fifteen hundred years ago, the courageous Princess Hemamali smuggled the sacred tooth of the Buddha into Ceylon. Now, for the first time, it is being brought to London to be part of a magnificent exhibit at the British Museum. But what if something were to happen to it? It would be a disaster for the British Empire. Sherlock Holmes, Dr. Watson, and even Mycroft Holmes are called upon to prevent such a crisis. This novella is inspired by the Sherlock Holmes mystery, The Sign of the Four.

A Sandal from East Anglia. Archeological excavations at an old abbey unearth an ancient document that has the potential to change the course of the British Empire and all of Christendom. Holmes encounters some evil young men and a strikingly beautiful young Sister, with a curious double life. The mystery is inspired by the original Sherlock Holmes story, *A Scandal in Bohemia*

The Bald-Headed Trust. Watson insists on taking Sherlock Holmes on a short vacation to the seaside in Plymouth. No sooner has Holmes arrived than he is needed to solve a double murder and prevent a massive fraud diabolically designed by the evil Professor himself. Who knew that a family of devout conservative churchgoers could come to the aid of Sherlock Holmes and bring enormous grief to evildoers? The story is inspired by *The Red-Headed League*.

A Case of Identity Theft. It is the fall of 1888, and Jack the Ripper is terrorizing London. A young married couple is found, minus their heads. Sherlock Holmes, Dr. Watson, the couple's mothers, and Mycroft must join forces to find the murderer before he kills again and makes off with half a million pounds. The novella is a tribute to A Case of Identity. It will appeal both to devoted fans of Sherlock Holmes, as well as to those who love the great game of rugby

The Hudson Valley Mystery. A young man in New York went mad and murdered his father. His mother believes he is innocent and knows he is not crazy. She appeals to Sherlock Holmes and, together with Dr. and Mrs. Watson, he crosses the Atlantic to help this client in need. This new story was inspired by *The Boscombe Valley*

The Mystery of the Five Oranges. A desperate father enters 221B Baker Street. His daughter has been kidnapped and spirited off to North America. The evil network who have taken her has spies everywhere. There is only one hope – Sherlock Holmes. Sherlockians will enjoy this new adventure, inspired by The Five Orange Pips and Anne of Green Gables.

The Man Who Was Twisted But Hip. France is torn apart by The Dreyfus Affair. Westminster needs Sherlock Holmes so that the evil tide of anti-Semitism that has engulfed France will not spread. Sherlock and Watson go to Paris to solve the mystery and thwart Moriarty. This new mystery is inspired by *The Man with the Twisted Lip,* as well as by *The Hunchback of Notre Dame*

The Adventure of the Blue Belt Buckle. A young street urchin discovers a man's belt and buckle under a bush in Hyde Park. A body is found in a hotel room in Mayfair. Scotland Yard seeks the help of Sherlock Holmes in solving the murder. The Queen's Jubilee could be ruined. Sherlock Holmes, Dr. Watson, Scotland Yard, and Her Majesty all team up to prevent a crime of unspeakable dimensions. A new mystery inspired by *The Blue Carbuncle.*

The Adventure of the Spectred Bat. A beautiful young woman, just weeks away from giving birth, arrives at Baker Street in the middle of the night. Her sister was attacked by a bat and died, and now it is attacking her. A vampire? The story is a tribute to *The Adventure of the Speckled Band* and, like the original, leaves the mind wondering and the heart racing.

The Adventure of the Engineer's Mom. A brilliant young Cambridge University engineer is carrying out secret research for the Admiralty. It will lead to the building of the world's most powerful battleship, The Dreadnaught. His adventuress mother is kidnapped, and he seeks the help of Sherlock Holmes. This new mystery is a tribute to *The Engineer's Thumb.*

www.SherlockHolmesMystery.com

The Adventure of the Notable Bachelorette. A snobbish nobleman enters 221B Baker Street, demanding the help in finding his much younger wife – a beautiful and spirited American from the West. Three days later, the wife is accused of a vile crime. Now she comes to Sherlock Holmes seeking to prove her innocence. This new mystery was inspired by *The Adventure of the Noble Bachelor.*

The Adventure of the Beryl Anarchists. A deeply distressed banker enters 221B Baker St. His safe has been robbed, and he is certain that his motorcycle-riding sons have betrayed him. Highly incriminating and embarrassing records of the financial and personal affairs of England's nobility are now in the hands of blackmailers. Then a young girl is murdered. A tribute to *The Adventure of the Beryl Coronet.*

The Adventure of the Coiffured Bitches. A beautiful young woman will soon inherit a lot of money. She disappears. Another young woman finds out far too much and, in desperation, seeks help. Sherlock Holmes, Dr. Watson, and Miss Violet Hunter must solve the mystery of the coiffured bitches and avoid the massive mastiff that could tear their throats out. A tribute to *The Adventure of the Copper Beeches*

The Silver Horse, Braised. The greatest horse race of the century will take place at Epsom Downs. Millions have been bet. Owners, jockeys, grooms, and gamblers from across England and America arrive. Jockeys and horses are killed. Holmes fails to solve the crime until… This mystery is a tribute to *Silver Blaze* and the great racetrack stories of Damon Runyon.

The Box of Cards. A brother and a sister from a strict religious family disappear. The parents are alarmed, but Scotland Yard says they are just off sowing their wild oats. A horrific, gruesome package arrives in the post, and it becomes clear that a terrible crime is in process. Sherlock Holmes is called in to help. A tribute to *The Cardboard Box*

The Yellow Farce. Sherlock Holmes is sent to Japan. The war between Russia and Japan is raging. Alliances between countries in these years before World War I are fragile, and any misstep could plunge the world into Armageddon. The wife of the British ambassador is suspected of being a Russian agent. Join Holmes and Watson as they travel around the world to Japan. Inspired by *The Yellow Face.*

The Stock Market Murders. A young man's friend has gone missing. Two more bodies of young men turn up. All are tied to The City and to one of the greatest frauds ever visited upon the citizens of England. The story is based on the true story of James Whitaker Wright and is inspired by *The Stock Broker's Clerk.* Any resemblance of the villain to a certain American political figure is entirely coincidental.

The Glorious Yacht. On the night of April 12, 1912, off the coast of Newfoundland, one of the greatest disasters of all time took place – the Unsinkable Titanic struck an iceberg and sank with a horrendous loss of life. The news of the disaster leads Holmes and Watson to reminisce about one of their earliest adventures. It began as a sailing race and ended as a tale of murder, kidnapping, piracy, and survival through a tempest. A tribute to *The Gloria Scott.*

www.SherlockHolmesMystery.com

A Most Grave Ritual. In 1649, King Charles I escaped and made a desperate run for Continent. Did he leave behind a vast fortune? The patriarch of an ancient Royalist family dies in the courtyard, and the locals believe that the headless ghost of the king did him in. The police accuse his son of murder. Sherlock Holmes is hired to exonerate the lad. A tribute to *The Musgrave Ritual*

The Spy Gate Liars. Dr. Watson receives an urgent telegram telling him that Sherlock Holmes is in France and near death. He rushes to aid his dear friend, only to find that what began as a doctor's housecall has turned into yet another adventure as Sherlock Holmes races to keep an unknown ruthless murderer from dispatching yet another former German army officer. A tribute to *The Reigate Squires.*

The Cuckold Man Colonel James Barclay needs the help of Sherlock Holmes. His exceptionally beautiful, but much younger, wife has disappeared, and foul play is suspected. Has she been kidnapped and held for ransom? Or is she in the clutches of a deviant monster? The story is a tribute not only to the original mystery, *The Crooked Man*, but also to the biblical story of King David and Bathsheba

The Impatient Dissidents. In March 1881, the Czar of Russia was assassinated by anarchists. That summer, an attempt was made to murder his daughter, Maria, the wife of England's Prince Alfred. A Russian Count is found dead in a hospital in London. Scotland Yard and the Home Office arrive at 221B and enlist the help of Sherlock Holmes to track down the killers and stop them. This new mystery is a tribute to *The Resident Patient.*

The Grecian, Earned. This story picks up where *The Greek Interpreter* left off. The villains of that story were murdered in Budapest, and so Holmes and Watson set off in search of "the Grecian girl" to solve the mystery. What they discover is a massive plot involving the re-birth of the Olympic games in 1896 and a colorful cast of characters at home and on the Continent.

The Three Rhodes Not Taken. Oxford University is famous for its passionate pursuit of learning. The Rhodes Scholarship has been recently established, and some men are prepared to lie, steal, slander, and, maybe murder, in the pursuit of it. Sherlock Holmes is called upon to track down a thief who has stolen vital documents pertaining to the winner of the scholarship, but what will he do when the prime suspect is found dead? A tribute to *The Three Students*

The Naval Knaves. On September 15, 1894, an anarchist attempted to bomb the Greenwich Observatory. He failed, but the attempt led Sherlock Holmes into an intricate web of spies, foreign naval officers, and a beautiful princess. Once again, suspicion landed on poor Percy Phelps, now working in a senior position in the Admiralty, and once again, Holmes has to use both his powers of deduction and raw courage to not only rescue Percy but to prevent an unspeakable disaster. A tribute to *The Naval Treaty*.

A Scandal in Trumplandia. NOT a new mystery but a political satire. The story is a parody of the much-loved original story, *A Scandal in Bohemia*, with the character of the King of Bohemia replaced by you-know-who. If you enjoy both political satire and Sherlock Holmes, you will get a chuckle out of this new story.

The Binomial Asteroid Problem. The deadly final encounter between Professor Moriarty and Sherlock Holmes took place at Reichenbach Falls. But when was their first encounter? This new story answers that question. What began a stolen Gladstone bag escalates into murder and more. This new story is a tribute to *The Adventure of the Final Problem.*

The Adventure of Charlotte Europa Golderton. *Charles Augustus Milverton* was shot and sent to his just reward. But now another diabolical scheme of blackmail has emerged centered in the telegraph offices of the Royal Mail. It is linked to an archeological expedition whose director disappeared. Someone is prepared to murder to protect their ill-gotten gain and possibly steal a priceless treasure. Holmes is hired by not one but three women who need his help.

The Mystery of 222 Baker Street. The body of a Scotland Yard inspector is found in a locked room in 222 Baker Street. There is no clue as to how he died. Then another murder in the very same room. Holmes and Watson might have to offer themselves as potential victims if the culprits are to be discovered. A tribute to the original Sherlock Holmes story, *The Adventure of the Empty House*

The Adventure of the Norwood Rembrandt. A man facing execution appeals to Sherlock Holmes to save him. He claims that he is innocent. Holmes agrees to take on his case. Five years ago, he was convicted of the largest theft of art masterpieces in British history, and of murdering the butler who tried to stop him. Holmes and Watson have to find the real murderer and the missing works of art --- if the client is innocent after all. A tribute to *The Adventure of the Norwood Builder* in the original Canon.

The Horror of the Bastard's Villa. A Scottish clergyman and his faithful border collie visit 221B and tell a tale of a ghostly Banshee on the Isle of Skye. After the specter appeared, two people died. Holmes sends Watson on ahead to investigate and report. More terrifying horrors occur, and Sherlock Holmes must come and solve the awful mystery before more people are murdered. A tribute to the original story in the Canon, Arthur Conan Doyle's masterpiece, *The Hound of the Baskervilles.*

The Dancer from the Dance. In 1909 the entire world of dance changed when Les Ballets Russes opened in Paris. They also made annual visits to the West End in London. Tragically, during their 1913 tour, two of their dancers are found murdered. Sherlock Holmes is brought into to find the murderer and prevent any more killings. The story adheres fairly closely to the history of ballet and is a tribute to the original story in the Canon, *The Adventure of the Dancing Men.*

The Solitary Bicycle Thief. Remember Violet Smith, the beautiful young woman whom Sherlock Holmes and Dr. Watson rescued from a forced marriage, as recorded in *The Adventure of the Solitary Cyclist?* Ten years later, she and Cyril reappear in 221B Baker Street with a strange tale of the theft of their bicycles. What on the surface seemed like a trifle turns out to be the door that leads Sherlock Holmes into a web of human trafficking, espionage, blackmail, and murder. A new and powerful cabal of master criminals has formed in London, and they will stop at nothing, not even the murder of an innocent foreign student, to extend the hold on the criminal underworld of London

www.SherlockHolmesMystery.com

The Adventure of the Prioress's Tale. The senior field hockey team from an elite girls' school goes to Dover for a beach holiday … and disappears. Have they been abducted into white slavery? Did they run off to Paris? Are they being held for ransom? Can Sherlock Holmes find them in time? Holmes, Watson, Lestrade, the Prioress of the school, and a new gang of Irregulars must find them before something terrible happens. a tribute to *The Adventure of the Priory School in the Canon.*

The Adventure of Mrs. J.L. Heber. A mad woman is murdering London bachelors by driving a railway spike through their heads. Scotland Yard demands that Sherlock Holmes help them find and stop a crazed murderess who is re-enacting the biblical murders by Jael. Holmes agrees and finds that revenge is being taken for deeds treachery and betrayal that took place ten years ago in the Rocky Mountains of Canada. Holmes, Watson, and Lestrade must move quickly before more men and women lose their lives. The story is a tribute to the original Sherlock Holmes story, *The Adventure of Black Peter.*

The Return of Napoleon. In October 1805, Napoleon's fleet was defeated in the Battle of Trafalgar. Now his ghost has returned to England for the centenary of the battle, intent on wreaking revenge on the descendants of Admiral Horatio Nelson and on all of England. The mother of the great-great-grandchildren of Admiral Nelson contacts Sherlock Holmes, needing his help. First, Dr. Watson comes to the manor, and he meets not only the lovely children but also finds that something apparently supernatural is going on. Holmes assumes that some mad Frenchmen, intent on avenging Napoleon, are conspiring to wreak havoc on England and possibly threatening the children. Watson believes that something terrifying and occult may be at work. Neither is prepared for the true target of the Napoleonists, or of the Emperor's ghost

The Adventure of the Pinched Palimpsest. A professor has been proselytizing for anarchism. Three students fall for his doctrines and engage in direct action by stealing priceless artifacts from the British Museum, returning them to the oppressed people from whom their colonial masters stole them. In the midst of their caper, a museum guard is shot dead, and they are charged with the murder. After being persuaded by a vulnerable friend of the students, Sherlock Holmes agrees to take on the case. He soon discovers that no one involved is telling the complete truth. Join Holmes and Watson as they race from London to Oxford, then to Cambridge and finally up to a remote village in Scotland and seek to discover the clues that are tied to an obscure medieval palimpsest.

The Adventure of the Missing Better Half. Did you ever wonder what happened to Godfrey Staunton, the missing Three-Quarter, after Holmes found him? This story tells you. He met an exceptional young woman, fell in love, and got married. He was chosen to play on England's National Team in the 1899 Home Nations Championship games. Life was good. ... and then it got much worse. Together -- Godfrey Staunton, Dr. Leslie Armstrong, Dr. Watson, and Sherlock Holmes -- must stop an unspeakable crime taking place. This 38th New Sherlock Holmes. A tribute to *The Adventure of the Missing Three Quarter.*

The Inequality of Mercy. What happened after Sherlock Holmes and Dr. Watson pardoned Captain Jack Croker for killing Sir Eustace at the Abbey Grange. Have you imagined that he sailed the seven seas for a year and then returned to his beautiful, beloved Mary Fraser? That didn't happen. A year later, murder, treachery, and international intrigue descended on Abbey Grange, and, once again, Sherlock Holmes was called upon to bring criminals to justice and assist in the course of true love. Buy the story now, and find out what happened.

The Adventure of the Second Entente. In June of 1901, a wealthy young nobleman is murdered, and yet again, Scotland Yard requires help from Sherlock Holmes. The baron has recently returned from an expedition searching for oil in Persia. His only relative and sole heir, a woman from California is the obvious suspect. But then she comes to Sherlock Holmes desperately seeking his help. If she did not kill the man, then who did? Join Holmes, Watson and an unusual woman as they seek to solve the crime and avoid becoming victims themselves. The story is a tribute to the original Sherlock Holmes mystery, *The Adventure of the Second Stain*.

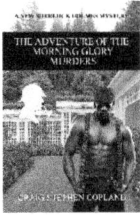

The Adventure of the Morning Glory Murders. Sherlock Holmes confronts the horrible racial and religious prejudice that was rampant in the Victorian era and helps the heroic victims of those evils discover a new life. A family from Argentina has disappeared and it is feared that they were abducted. Their lives are in danger. The father, a colonel in the Argentine army has enemies from years ago that may be seeking revenge. The gigantic 'mulatto' who was the cook in the story about Wisteria Lodge (remember him?) is falsely accused. With his help, Sherlock Holmes must find the family before it is too late. If reading about the prejudices of the Victorian era -- many of which appeared in the original Sherlock Holmes stories -- upsets you, this is not for you. However, if you want to read about how brave people faced those evils and overcame them, this is a story you will enjoy.

The Adventure of the Treacherous Trust. A beautiful, brilliant young woman attracts the attention of a wealthy, older gentleman. He insists that she join the board of directors of a popular charity, run by his son. A meeting of the directors is held at the family estate. She attends and quarrels with the son. An hour later, she falls off the roof terrace. Nobody can believe that her death is anything but a tragic accident. Nobody, that is, except her sister, Miss Violet Westbury. She comes to Sherlock Holmes seeking his help and together they and Dr. Watson try to discern what happened to her sister. The story travels all the way to Calcutta and back to St. James Square, and the villains almost get away with their vile crime ... almost. A tribute the *The Adventure of the Bruce-Partington Plans.*

www.SherlockHolmesMystery.com

Contributions to the Great Game of Sherlockian Scholarship

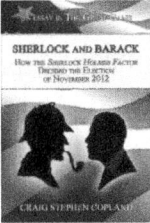

Sherlock and Barack. This is NOT a new Sherlock Holmes Mystery. It is a Sherlockian research monograph. Why did Barack Obama win in November 2012? Why did Mitt Romney lose? Pundits and political scientists have offered countless reasons. This book reveals the truth - The Sherlock Holmes Factor. Had it not been for Sherlock Holmes, Mitt Romney would be president.

From The Beryl Coronet to Vimy Ridge. This is NOT a New Sherlock Holmes Mystery. It is a monograph of Sherlockian research. This new monograph in the Great Game of Sherlockian scholarship argues that there was a Sherlock Holmes factor in the causes of World War I... and that it is secretly revealed in the *roman a clef* story that we know as *The Adventure of the Beryl Coronet*

www.SherlockHolmesMystery.com

Reverend Ezekiel Black—
The Sherlock Holmes of the American West

A Scarlet Trail of Murder. At ten o'clock on Sunday morning, the twenty-second of October, 1882, in an abandoned house in the West Bottom of Kansas City, a fellow named Jasper Harrison did not wake up. His inability to do was the result of his having had his throat cut. The Reverend Mr. Ezekiel Black, a part-time Methodist minister, and an itinerant US Marshall is called in. This original western mystery was inspired by the great Sherlock Holmes classic, *A Study in Scarlet*

The Brand of the Flying Four. This case all began one quiet evening in a room in Kansas City. A few weeks later, a gruesome murder, took place in Denver. By the time Rev. Black had solved the mystery, justice, of the frontier variety, not the courtroom, had been meted out. The story is inspired by *The Sign of the Four* by Arthur Conan Doyle, and like that story, it combines murder most foul, and romance most enticing.

www.SherlockHolmesMystery.com

Collection Sets for eBooks and paperback are available at *40% off the price of buying them separately.*

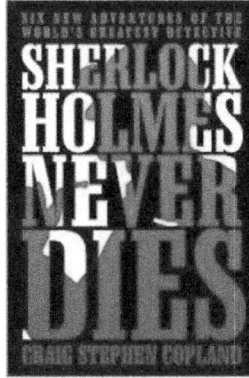

Collection One

The Sign of the Tooth
The Hudson Valley Mystery
A Case of Identity Theft
The Bald-Headed Trust
Studying Scarlet
The Mystery of the Five Oranges

Collection Two

A Sandal from East Anglia
The Man Who Was Twisted But Hip
The Blue Belt Buckle
The Spectred Bat

Collection Three

The Engineer's Mom
The Notable Bachelorette
The Beryl Anarchists
The Coiffured Bitches

Collection Four

The Silver Horse, Braised
The Box of Cards
The Yellow Farce
The Three Rhodes Not Taken

Collection Five

The Stock Market Murders
The Glorious Yacht
The Most Grave Ritual
The Spy Gate Liars

Collection Six

The Cuckold Man
The Impatient Dissidents
The Grecian, Earned
The Naval Knaves

Collection Seven

The Binomial Asteroid Problem
The Mystery of 222 Baker Street
The Adventure of Charlotte Europa Golderton
The Adventure of the Norwood Rembrandt

Collection Eight

The Dancer from the Dance
The Adventure of the Prioress's Tale
The Adventure of Mrs. J. L. Heber
The Solitary Bicycle Thief

Collection Nine

Super Collections A and B

40 New Sherlock Holmes Mysteries.

The perfect ebooks for readers who can only borrow one book a month from Amazon

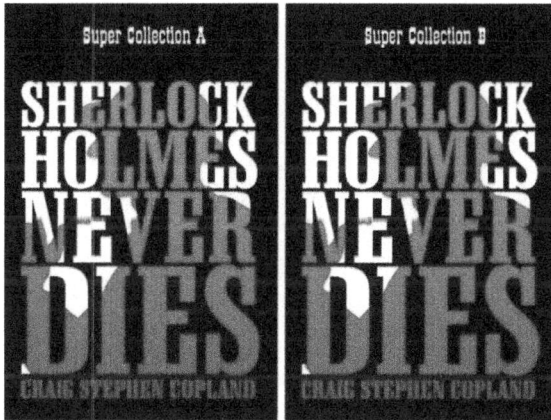

www.SherlockHolmesMystery.com

The Adventure of the Devil's Foot

The Original Sherlock Holmes Story

Arthur Conan Doyle

The Adventure of the Devil's Foot

In recording from time to time some of the curious experiences and interesting recollections which I associate with my long and intimate friendship with Mr. Sherlock Holmes, I have continually been faced by difficulties caused by his own aversion to publicity. To his sombre and cynical spirit all popular applause was always abhorrent, and nothing amused him more at the end of a successful case than to hand over the actual exposure to some orthodox official, and to listen with a mocking smile to the general chorus of misplaced congratulation. It was indeed this attitude upon the part of my friend and certainly not any lack of interesting material which has caused me of late years to lay very few of my records before the public. My participation in some if his adventures was always a privilege which entailed discretion and reticence upon me.

It was, then, with considerable surprise that I received a telegram from Homes last Tuesday—he has never been known to write where a telegram would serve—in the following terms:

Why not tell them of the Cornish horror—strangest case I have handled.

I have no idea what backward sweep of memory had brought the matter fresh to his mind, or what freak had caused him to desire that I should recount it; but I hasten, before another cancelling telegram may arrive, to hunt out the notes which give me the exact details of the case and to lay the narrative before my readers.

It was, then, in the spring of the year 1897 that Holmes's iron constitution showed some symptoms of giving way in the face of constant hard work of a most exacting kind, aggravated, perhaps, by occasional indiscretions of his own. In March of that year Dr. Moore Agar, of Harley Street, whose dramatic introduction to Holmes I may some day recount, gave positive injunctions that the famous private agent lay aside all his cases and surrender himself to complete rest if he wished to avert an absolute breakdown. The state of his health was not a matter in which he himself took the faintest interest, for his mental detachment was absolute, but he was induced at last, on the threat of being permanently disqualified from work, to give himself a complete change of scene and air. Thus it was that in the early spring of that year we found ourselves together in a small cottage near Poldhu Bay, at the further extremity of the Cornish peninsula.

It was a singular spot, and one peculiarly well suited to the grim humour of my patient. From the windows of our little whitewashed house, which stood high upon a grassy headland, we looked down upon the whole sinister semicircle of Mounts Bay, that old death trap of sailing vessels, with its fringe of black cliffs and surge-swept reefs on which innumerable seamen have met their end. With a northerly breeze it lies placid and sheltered, inviting the storm-tossed craft to tack into it for rest and protection.

Then come the sudden swirl round of the wind, the blistering gale from the south-west, the dragging anchor, the lee shore, and the last battle in the creaming breakers. The wise mariner stands far out from that evil place.

On the land side our surroundings were as sombre as on the sea. It was a country of rolling moors, lonely and dun-colored, with an occasional church tower to mark the site of some old-world village. In every direction upon these moors there were traces of some vanished race which had passed utterly away, and left as it sole record strange monuments of stone, irregular mounds which contained the burned ashes of the dead, and curious earthworks which hinted at prehistoric strife. The glamour and mystery of the place, with its sinister atmosphere of forgotten nations, appealed to the imagination of my friend, and he spent much of his time in long walks and solitary meditations upon the moor. The ancient Cornish language had also arrested his attention, and he had, I remember, conceived the idea that it was akin to the Chaldean, and had been largely derived from the Phoenician traders in tin. He had received a consignment of books upon philology and was settling down to develop this thesis when suddenly, to my sorrow and to his unfeigned delight, we found ourselves, even in that land of dreams, plunged into a problem at our very doors which was more intense, more engrossing, and infinitely more mysterious than any of those which had driven us from London. Our simple life and peaceful, healthy routine were violently interrupted, and we were precipitated into the midst of a series of events which caused the utmost excitement not only in Cornwall but throughout the whole west of England. Many of my readers may retain some recollection of what was called at the time "The Cornish Horror," though a most imperfect account of the matter reached the London press. Now, after thirteen years, I will give the true details of this inconceivable affair to the public.

I have said that scattered towers marked the villages which dotted this part of Cornwall. The nearest of these was the hamlet of Tredannick Wollas, where the cottages of a couple of hundred inhabitants clustered round an ancient, moss-grown church. The vicar of the parish, Mr. Roundhay, was something of an archaeologist, and as such Holmes had made his acquaintance. He was a middle-aged man, portly and affable, with a considerable fund of local lore. At his invitation we had taken tea at the vicarage and had come to know, also, Mr. Mortimer Tregennis, an independent gentleman, who increased the clergyman's scanty resources by taking rooms in his large, straggling house. The vicar, being a bachelor, was glad to come to such an arrangement, though he had little in common with his lodger, who was a thin, dark, spectacled man, with a stoop which gave the impression of actual, physical deformity. I remember that during our short visit we found the vicar garrulous, but his lodger strangely reticent, a sad-faced, introspective man, sitting with averted eyes, brooding apparently upon his own affairs.

These were the two men who entered abruptly into our little sitting-room on Tuesday, March the 16th, shortly after our breakfast hour, as we were smoking together, preparatory to our daily excursion upon the moors.

"Mr. Holmes," said the vicar in an agitated voice, "the most extraordinary and tragic affair has occurred during the night. It is the most unheard-of business. We can only regard it as a special Providence that you should chance to be here at the time, for in all England you are the one man we need."

I glared at the intrusive vicar with no very friendly eyes; but Holmes took his pipe from his lips and sat up in his chair like an old hound who hears the view-halloa. He waved his hand to the sofa, and our palpitating visitor with his agitated companion sat side by side upon it. Mr. Mortimer Tregennis was more self-contained than the clergyman, but the twitching of his thin hands and the brightness of his dark eyes showed that they shared a common emotion.

"Shall I speak or you?" he asked of the vicar.

"Well, as you seem to have made the discovery, whatever it may be, and the vicar to have had it second-hand, perhaps you had better do the speaking," said Holmes.

I glanced at the hastily clad clergyman, with the formally dressed lodger seated beside him, and was amused at the surprise which Holmes's simple deduction had brought to their faces.

"Perhaps I had best say a few words first," said the vicar, "and then you can judge if you will listen to the details from Mr. Tregennis, or whether we should not hasten at once to the scene of this mysterious affair. I may explain, then, that our friend here spent last evening in the company of his two brothers, Owen and George, and of his sister Brenda, at their house of Tredannick Wartha, which is near the old stone cross upon the moor. He left them shortly after ten o'clock, playing cards round the dining-room table, in excellent health and spirits. This morning, being an early riser, he walked in that direction before breakfast and was overtaken by the carriage of Dr. Richards, who explained that he had just been sent for on a most urgent call to Tredannick Wartha. Mr. Mortimer Tregennis naturally went with him. When he arrived at Tredannick Wartha he found an extraordinary state of things. His two brothers and his sister were seated round the table exactly as he had left them, the cards still spread in front of them and the candles burned down to their sockets. The sister lay back stone-dead in her chair, while the two brothers sat on each side of her laughing, shouting, and singing, the senses stricken clean out of them. All three of them, the dead woman and the two demented men, retained upon their faces an expression of the utmost horror—a convulsion of terror which was dreadful to look upon. There was no sign of the presence of anyone in the house, except Mrs. Porter, the old cook and housekeeper, who declared that she had slept deeply and heard no sound during the night. Nothing had been stolen or disarranged, and there is absolutely no explanation of what the horror can be which has frightened a woman to death and two strong men out of their senses. There is the situation, Mr. Holmes, in a nutshell, and if you can help us to clear it up you will have done a great work."

I had hoped that in some way I could coax my companion back into the quiet which had been the object of our journey; but one glance at his intense face and contracted eyebrows told me how vain was now the expectation. He sat for some little time in silence, absorbed in the strange drama which had broken in upon our peace.

"I will look into this matter," he said at last. "On the face of it, it would appear to be a case of a very exceptional nature. Have you been there yourself, Mr. Roundhay?"

"No, Mr. Holmes. Mr. Tregennis brought back the account to the vicarage, and I at once hurried over with him to consult you."

"How far is it to the house where this singular tragedy occurred?"

"About a mile inland."

"Then we shall walk over together. But before we start I must ask you a few questions, Mr. Mortimer Tregennis."

The other had been silent all this time, but I had observed that his more controlled excitement was even greater than the obtrusive emotion of the clergyman. He sat with a pale, drawn face, his anxious gaze fixed upon Holmes, and his thin hands clasped convulsively together. His pale lips quivered as he listened to the dreadful experience which had befallen his family, and his dark eyes seemed to reflect something of the horror of the scene.

"Ask what you like, Mr. Holmes," said he eagerly. "It is a bad thing to speak of, but I will answer you the truth."

"Tell me about last night."

"Well, Mr. Holmes, I supped there, as the vicar has said, and my elder brother George proposed a game of whist afterwards. We sat down about nine o'clock. It was a quarter-past ten when I moved to go. I left them all round the table, as merry as could be."

"Who let you out?"

"Mrs. Porter had gone to bed, so I let myself out. I shut the hall door behind me. The window of the room in which they sat was closed, but the blind was not drawn down. There was no change in door or window this morning, or any reason to think that any stranger had been to the house. Yet there they sat, driven clean mad with terror, and Brenda lying dead of fright, with her head hanging over the arm of the chair. I'll never get the sight of that room out of my mind so long as I live."

"The facts, as you state them, are certainly most remarkable," said Holmes. "I take it that you have no theory yourself which can in any way account for them?"

"It's devilish, Mr. Holmes, devilish!" cried Mortimer Tregennis. "It is not of this world. Something has come into that room which has dashed the light of reason from their minds. What human contrivance could do that?"

"I fear," said Holmes, "that if the matter is beyond humanity it is certainly beyond me. Yet we must exhaust all natural explanations before we fall back upon such a theory as this. As to yourself, Mr. Tregennis, I take it you were divided in some way from your family, since they lived together and you had rooms apart?"

"That is so, Mr. Holmes, though the matter is past and done with. We were a family of tin-miners at Redruth, but we sold our venture to a company, and so retired with enough to keep us. I won't deny that there was some feeling about the division of the money and it stood between us for a time, but it was all forgiven and forgotten, and we were the best of friends together."

"Looking back at the evening which you spent together, does anything stand out in your memory as throwing any possible light upon the tragedy? Think carefully, Mr. Tregennis, for any clue which can help me."

"There is nothing at all, sir."

"Your people were in their usual spirits?"

"Never better."

"Were they nervous people? Did they ever show any apprehension of coming danger?"

"Nothing of the kind."

"You have nothing to add then, which could assist me?"

Mortimer Tregennis considered earnestly for a moment.

"There is one thing occurs to me," said he at last. "As we sat at the table my back was to the window, and my brother George, he being my partner at cards, was facing it. I saw him once look hard over my shoulder, so I turned round and looked also. The blind was up and the window shut, but I could just make out the bushes on the lawn, and it seemed to me for a moment that I saw something moving among them. I couldn't even say if it was man or animal, but I just thought there was something there. When I asked him what he was looking at, he told me that he had the same feeling. That is all that I can say."

"Did you not investigate?"

"No; the matter passed as unimportant."

"You left them, then, without any premonition of evil?"

"None at all."

"I am not clear how you came to hear the news so early this morning."

"I am an early riser and generally take a walk before breakfast. This morning I had hardly started when the doctor in his carriage overtook me. He told me that old Mrs. Porter had sent a boy down with an urgent message. I sprang in beside him and we drove on. When we got there we looked into that dreadful room. The candles and the fire must have burned out hours before, and they had been sitting there in the dark until dawn had broken. The doctor said Brenda must have been dead at least six hours. There were no signs of violence. She just lay across the arm of the chair with that look on her face. George and Owen were singing snatches of songs and gibbering like two great apes. Oh, it was awful to see! I couldn't stand it, and the doctor was as white as a sheet. Indeed, he fell into a chair in a sort of faint, and we nearly had him on our hands as well."

"Remarkable—most remarkable!" said Holmes, rising and taking his hat. "I think, perhaps, we had better go down to Tredannick Wartha without further delay. I confess that I have seldom known a case which at first sight presented a more singular problem."

Our proceedings of that first morning did little to advance the investigation. It was marked, however, at the outset by an incident which left the most sinister impression upon my mind. The approach to the spot at which the tragedy occurred is down a narrow, winding, country lane. While we made our way along it we heard the rattle of a carriage coming towards us and stood aside to let it pass. As it drove by us I caught a glimpse through the closed window of a horribly contorted, grinning face glaring out at us. Those staring eyes and gnashing teeth flashed past us like a dreadful vision.

"My brothers!" cried Mortimer Tregennis, white to his lips. "They are taking them to Helston."

We looked with horror after the black carriage, lumbering upon its way. Then we turned our steps towards this ill-omened house in which they had met their strange fate.

It was a large and bright dwelling, rather a villa than a cottage, with a considerable garden which was already, in that Cornish air, well filled with spring flowers. Towards this garden the window of the sitting-room fronted, and from it, according to Mortimer Tregennis, must have come that thing of evil which had by sheer horror in a single instant blasted their minds. Holmes walked slowly and thoughtfully among the flower- plots and along the path before we entered the porch. So absorbed was he in his thoughts, I remember, that he stumbled over the watering-pot, upset its contents, and deluged both our feet and the garden path. Inside the house we were met by the elderly Cornish housekeeper, Mrs. Porter, who, with the aid of a young girl, looked after the wants of the family. She readily answered all Holmes's questions. She had heard nothing in the night. Her employers had all been in excellent spirits lately, and she had never known them more cheerful and prosperous. She had fainted with horror upon entering the room in the morning and seeing that dreadful company round the table. She had, when she recovered, thrown open the window to let the morning air in, and had run down to the lane, whence she sent a farm-lad for the doctor. The lady was on her bed upstairs if we cared to see her. It took four strong men to get the brothers into the asylum carriage. She would not herself stay in the house another day and was starting that very afternoon to rejoin her family at St. Ives.

We ascended the stairs and viewed the body. Miss Brenda Tregennis had been a very beautiful girl, though now verging upon middle age. Her dark, clear-cut face was handsome, even in death, but there still lingered upon it something of that convulsion of horror which had been her last human emotion. From her bedroom we descended to the sitting-room, where this strange tragedy had actually occurred. The charred ashes of the overnight fire lay in the grate. On the table were the four guttered and burned-out candles, with the cards scattered over its surface. The chairs had been moved back against the walls, but all else was as it had been the night before. Holmes paced with light, swift steps about the room; he sat in the various chairs, drawing them up and reconstructing their positions. He tested how much of the garden was visible; he examined the floor, the ceiling, and the fireplace; but never once did I see that sudden brightening of his eyes and tightening of his lips which would have told me that he saw some gleam of light in this utter darkness.

"Why a fire?" he asked once. "Had they always a fire in this small room on a spring evening?"

Mortimer Tregennis explained that the night was cold and damp. For that reason, after his arrival, the fire was lit. "What are you going to do now, Mr. Holmes?" he asked.

My friend smiled and laid his hand upon my arm. "I think, Watson, that I shall resume that course of tobacco-poisoning which you have so often and so justly condemned," said he. "With your permission, gentlemen, we will now return to our cottage, for I am not aware that any new factor is likely to come to our notice here. I will turn the facts over in my mind, Mr. Tregennis, and should anything occur to me I will certainly communicate with you and the vicar. In the meantime I wish you both good-morning."

It was not until long after we were back in Poldhu Cottage that Holmes broke his complete and absorbed silence. He sat coiled in his armchair, his haggard and ascetic face hardly visible amid the blue swirl of his tobacco smoke, his black brows drawn down, his forehead contracted, his eyes vacant and far away. Finally he laid down his pipe and sprang to his feet.

"It won't do, Watson!" said he with a laugh. "Let us walk along the cliffs together and search for flint arrows. We are more likely to find them than clues to this problem. To let the brain work without sufficient material is like racing an engine. It racks itself to pieces. The sea air, sunshine, and patience, Watson—all else will come.

"Now, let us calmly define our position, Watson," he continued as we skirted the cliffs together. "Let us get a firm grip of the very little which we DO know, so that when fresh facts arise we may be ready to fit them into their places. I take it, in the first place, that neither of us is prepared to admit diabolical intrusions into the affairs of men. Let us begin by ruling that entirely out of our minds. Very good. There remain three persons who have been grievously stricken by some conscious or unconscious human agency. That is firm ground. Now, when did this occur? Evidently, assuming his narrative to be true, it was immediately after Mr. Mortimer Tregennis had left the room. That is a very important point. The presumption is that it was within a few minutes afterwards. The cards still lay upon the table. It was already past their usual hour for bed. Yet they had not changed their position or pushed back their chairs. I repeat, then, that the occurrence was immediately after his departure, and not later than eleven o'clock last night.

"Our next obvious step is to check, so far as we can, the movements of Mortimer Tregennis after he left the room. In this there is no difficulty, and they seem to be above suspicion. Knowing my methods as you do, you were, of course, conscious of the somewhat clumsy water-pot expedient by which I obtained a clearer impress of his foot than might otherwise have been possible. The wet, sandy path took it admirably. Last night was also wet, you will remember, and it was not difficult—having obtained a sample print—to pick out his track among others and to follow his movements. He appears to have walked away swiftly in the direction of the vicarage.

"If, then, Mortimer Tregennis disappeared from the scene, and yet some outside person affected the card-players, how can we reconstruct that person, and how was such an impression of horror conveyed? Mrs. Porter may be eliminated. She is evidently harmless. Is there any evidence that someone crept up to the garden window and in some manner produced so terrific an effect that he drove those who saw it out of their senses? The only suggestion in this direction comes from Mortimer Tregennis himself, who says that his brother spoke about some movement in the garden. That is certainly remarkable, as the night was rainy, cloudy, and dark. Anyone who had the design to alarm these people would be compelled to place his very face against the glass before he could be seen. There is a three-foot flower- border outside this window, but no indication of a footmark. It is difficult to imagine, then, how an outsider could have made so terrible an impression upon the company, nor have we found any possible motive for so strange and elaborate an attempt. You perceive our difficulties, Watson?"

"They are only too clear," I answered with conviction.

"And yet, with a little more material, we may prove that they are not insurmountable," said Holmes. "I fancy that among your extensive archives, Watson, you may find some which were nearly as obscure. Meanwhile, we shall put the case aside until more accurate data are available, and devote the rest of our morning to the pursuit of neolithic man."

I may have commented upon my friend's power of mental detachment, but never have I wondered at it more than upon that spring morning in Cornwall when for two hours he discoursed upon celts, arrowheads, and shards, as lightly as if no sinister mystery were waiting for his solution. It was not until we had returned in the afternoon to our cottage that we found a visitor awaiting us, who soon brought our minds back to the matter in hand. Neither of us needed to be told who that visitor was. The huge body, the craggy and deeply seamed face with the fierce eyes and hawk-like nose, the grizzled hair which nearly brushed our cottage ceiling, the beard—golden at the fringes and white near the lips, save for the nicotine stain from his perpetual cigar—all these were as well known in London as in Africa, and could only be associated with the tremendous personality of Dr. Leon Sterndale, the great lion-hunter and explorer.

We had heard of his presence in the district and had once or twice caught sight of his tall figure upon the moorland paths. He made no advances to us, however, nor would we have dreamed of doing so to him, as it was well known that it was his love of seclusion which caused him to spend the greater part of the intervals between his journeys in a small bungalow buried in the lonely wood of Beauchamp Arriance. Here, amid his books and his maps, he lived an absolutely lonely life, attending to his own simple wants and paying little apparent heed to the affairs of his neighbours. It was a surprise to me, therefore, to hear him asking Holmes in an eager voice whether he had made any advance in his reconstruction of this mysterious episode. "The county police are utterly at fault," said he, "but perhaps your wider experience has suggested some conceivable explanation. My only claim to being taken into your confidence is that during my many residences here I have come to know this family of Tregennis very well—indeed, upon my Cornish mother's side I could call them cousins—and their strange fate has naturally been a great shock to me. I may tell you that I had got as far as Plymouth upon my way to Africa, but the news reached me this morning, and I came straight back again to help in the inquiry."

Holmes raised his eyebrows.

"Did you lose your boat through it?"

"I will take the next."

"Dear me! that is friendship indeed."

"I tell you they were relatives."

"Quite so—cousins of your mother. Was your baggage aboard the ship?"

"Some of it, but the main part at the hotel."

"I see. But surely this event could not have found its way into the Plymouth morning papers."

"No, sir; I had a telegram."

"Might I ask from whom?"

A shadow passed over the gaunt face of the explorer.

"You are very inquisitive, Mr. Holmes."

"It is my business."

With an effort Dr. Sterndale recovered his ruffled composure.

"I have no objection to telling you," he said. "It was Mr. Roundhay, the vicar, who sent me the telegram which recalled me."

"Thank you," said Holmes. "I may say in answer to your original question that I have not cleared my mind entirely on the subject of this case, but that I have every hope of reaching some conclusion. It would be premature to say more."

"Perhaps you would not mind telling me if your suspicions point in any particular direction?"

"No, I can hardly answer that."

"Then I have wasted my time and need not prolong my visit." The famous doctor strode out of our cottage in considerable ill- humour, and within five minutes Holmes had followed him. I saw him no more until the evening, when he returned with a slow step and haggard face which assured me that he had made no great progress with his investigation. He glanced at a telegram which awaited him and threw it into the grate.

"From the Plymouth hotel, Watson," he said. "I learned the name of it from the vicar, and I wired to make certain that Dr. Leon Sterndale's account was true. It appears that he did indeed spend last night there, and that he has actually allowed some of his baggage to go on to Africa, while he returned to be present at this investigation. What do you make of that, Watson?"

"He is deeply interested."

"Deeply interested—yes. There is a thread here which we had not yet grasped and which might lead us through the tangle. Cheer up, Watson, for I am very sure that our material has not yet all come to hand. When it does we may soon leave our difficulties behind us."

Little did I think how soon the words of Holmes would be realized, or how strange and sinister would be that new development which opened up an entirely fresh line of investigation. I was shaving at my window in the morning when I heard the rattle of hoofs and, looking up, saw a dog-cart coming at a gallop down the road. It pulled up at our door, and our friend, the vicar, sprang from it and rushed up our garden path. Holmes was already dressed, and we hastened down to meet him.

Our visitor was so excited that he could hardly articulate, but at last in gasps and bursts his tragic story came out of him.

"We are devil-ridden, Mr. Holmes! My poor parish is devil-ridden!" he cried. "Satan himself is loose in it! We are given over into his hands!" He danced about in his agitation, a ludicrous object if it were not for his ashy face and startled eyes. Finally he shot out his terrible news.

"Mr. Mortimer Tregennis died during the night, and with exactly the same symptoms as the rest of his family."

Holmes sprang to his feet, all energy in an instant.

"Can you fit us both into your dog-cart?"

"Yes, I can."

"Then, Watson, we will postpone our breakfast. Mr. Roundhay, we are entirely at your disposal. Hurry—hurry, before things get disarranged."

The lodger occupied two rooms at the vicarage, which were in an angle by themselves, the one above the other. Below was a large sitting-room; above, his bedroom. They looked out upon a croquet lawn which came up to the windows. We had arrived before the doctor or the police, so that everything was absolutely undisturbed. Let me describe exactly the scene as we saw it upon that misty March morning. It has left an impression which can never be effaced from my mind.

The atmosphere of the room was of a horrible and depressing stuffiness. The servant had first entered had thrown up the window, or it would have been even more intolerable. This might partly be due to the fact that a lamp stood flaring and smoking on the centre table. Beside it sat the dead man, leaning back in his chair, his thin beard projecting, his spectacles pushed up on to his forehead, and his lean dark face turned towards the window and twisted into the same distortion of terror which had marked the features of his dead sister. His limbs were convulsed and his fingers contorted as though he had died in a very paroxysm of fear. He was fully clothed, though there were signs that his dressing had been done in a hurry. We had already learned that his bed had been slept in, and that the tragic end had come to him in the early morning.

One realized the red-hot energy which underlay Holmes's phlegmatic exterior when one saw the sudden change which came over him from the moment that he entered the fatal apartment. In an instant he was tense and alert, his eyes shining, his face set, his limbs quivering with eager activity. He was out on the lawn, in through the window, round the room, and up into the bedroom, for all the world like a dashing foxhound drawing a cover. In the bedroom he made a rapid cast around and ended by throwing open the window, which appeared to give him some fresh cause for excitement, for he leaned out of it with loud ejaculations of interest and delight. Then he rushed down the stair, out through the open window, threw himself upon his face on the lawn, sprang up and into the room once more, all with the energy of the hunter who is at the very heels of his quarry. The lamp, which was an ordinary standard, he examined with minute care, making certain measurements upon its bowl. He carefully scrutinized with his lens the talc shield which covered the top of the chimney and scraped off some ashes which adhered to its upper surface, putting some of them into an envelope, which he placed in his pocketbook. Finally, just as the doctor and the official police put in an appearance, he beckoned to the vicar and we all three went out upon the lawn.

"I am glad to say that my investigation has not been entirely barren," he remarked. "I cannot remain to discuss the matter with the police, but I should be exceedingly obliged, Mr. Roundhay, if you would give the inspector my compliments and direct his attention to the bedroom window and to the sitting- room lamp. Each is suggestive, and together they are almost conclusive. If the police would desire further information I shall be happy to see any of them at the cottage. And now, Watson, I think that, perhaps, we shall be better employed elsewhere."

It may be that the police resented the intrusion of an amateur, or that they imagined themselves to be upon some hopeful line of investigation; but it is certain that we heard nothing from them for the next two days. During this time Holmes spent some of his time smoking and dreaming in the cottage; but a greater portion in country walks which he undertook alone, returning after many hours without remark as to where he had been. One experiment served to show me the line of his investigation. He had bought a lamp which was the duplicate of the one which had burned in the room of Mortimer Tregennis on the morning of the tragedy. This he filled with the same oil as that used at the vicarage, and he carefully timed the period which it would take to be exhausted. Another experiment which he made was of a more unpleasant nature, and one which I am not likely ever to forget.

"You will remember, Watson," he remarked one afternoon, "that there is a single common point of resemblance in the varying reports which have reached us. This concerns the effect of the atmosphere of the room in each case upon those who had first entered it. You will recollect that Mortimer Tregennis, in describing the episode of his last visit to his brother's house, remarked that the doctor on entering the room fell into a chair? You had forgotten? Well I can answer for it that it was so. Now, you will remember also that Mrs. Porter, the housekeeper, told us that she herself fainted upon entering the room and had afterwards opened the window. In the second case—that of Mortimer Tregennis himself—you cannot have forgotten the horrible stuffiness of the room when we arrived, though the servant had thrown open the window. That servant, I found upon inquiry, was so ill that she had gone to her bed. You will admit, Watson, that these facts are very suggestive. In each case there is evidence of a poisonous atmosphere. In each case, also, there is combustion going on in the room—in the one case a fire, in the other a lamp. The fire was needed, but the lamp was lit—as a comparison of the oil consumed will show—long after it was broad daylight. Why? Surely because there is some connection between three things—the burning, the stuffy atmosphere, and, finally, the madness or death of those unfortunate people. That is clear, is it not?"

"It would appear so."

"At least we may accept it as a working hypothesis. We will suppose, then, that something was burned in each case which produced an atmosphere causing strange toxic effects. Very good. In the first instance—that of the Tregennis family—this substance was placed in the fire. Now the window was shut, but the fire would naturally carry fumes to some extent up the chimney. Hence one would expect the effects of the poison to be less than in the second case, where there was less escape for the vapour. The result seems to indicate that it was so, since in the first case only the woman, who had presumably the more sensitive organism, was killed, the others exhibiting that temporary or permanent lunacy which is evidently the first effect of the drug. In the second case the result was complete. The facts, therefore, seem to bear out the theory of a poison which worked by combustion.

"With this train of reasoning in my head I naturally looked about in Mortimer Tregennis's room to find some remains of this substance. The obvious place to look was the talc shelf or smoke-guard of the lamp. There, sure enough, I perceived a number of flaky ashes, and round the edges a fringe of brownish powder, which had not yet been consumed. Half of this I took, as you saw, and I placed it in an envelope."

"Why half, Holmes?"

"It is not for me, my dear Watson, to stand in the way of the official police force. I leave them all the evidence which I found. The poison still remained upon the talc had they the wit to find it. Now, Watson, we will light our lamp; we will, however, take the precaution to open our window to avoid the premature decease of two deserving members of society, and you will seat yourself near that open window in an armchair unless, like a sensible man, you determine to have nothing to do with the affair. Oh, you will see it out, will you? I thought I knew my Watson. This chair I will place opposite yours, so that we may be the same distance from the poison and face to face. The door we will leave ajar. Each is now in a position to watch the other and to bring the experiment to an end should the symptoms seem alarming. Is that all clear? Well, then, I take our powder—or what remains of it—from the envelope, and I lay it above the burning lamp. So! Now, Watson, let us sit down and await developments."

They were not long in coming. I had hardly settled in my chair before I was conscious of a thick, musky odour, subtle and nauseous. At the very first whiff of it my brain and my imagination were beyond all control. A thick, black cloud swirled before my eyes, and my mind told me that in this cloud, unseen as yet, but about to spring out upon my appalled senses, lurked all that was vaguely horrible, all that was monstrous and inconceivably wicked in the universe. Vague shapes swirled and swam amid the dark cloud-bank, each a menace and a warning of something coming, the advent of some unspeakable dweller upon the threshold, whose very shadow would blast my soul. A freezing horror took possession of me. I felt that my hair was rising, that my eyes were protruding, that my mouth was opened, and my tongue like leather. The turmoil within my brain was such that something must surely snap. I tried to scream and was vaguely aware of some hoarse croak which was my own voice, but distant and detached from myself At the same moment, in some effort of escape, I broke through that cloud of despair and had a glimpse of Holmes's face, white, rigid, and drawn with horror—the very look which I had seen upon the features of the dead. It was that vision which gave me an instant of sanity and of strength. I dashed from my chair, threw my arms round Holmes, and together we lurched through the door, and an instant afterwards had thrown ourselves down upon the grass plot and were lying side by side, conscious only of the glorious sunshine which was bursting its way through the hellish cloud of terror which had girt us in. Slowly it rose from our souls like the mists from a landscape until peace and reason had returned, and we were sitting upon the grass, wiping our clammy foreheads, and looking with apprehension at each other to mark the last traces of that terrific experience which we had undergone.

"Upon my word, Watson!" said Holmes at last with an unsteady voice, "I owe you both my thanks and an apology. It was an unjustifiable experiment even for one's self, and doubly so for a friend. I am really very sorry."

"You know," I answered with some emotion, for I have never seen so much of Holmes's heart before, "that it is my greatest joy and privilege to help you."

He relapsed at once into the half-humorous, half-cynical vein which was his habitual attitude to those about him. "It would be superfluous to drive us mad, my dear Watson," said he. "A candid observer would certainly declare that we were so already before we embarked upon so wild an experiment. I confess that I never imagined that the effect could be so sudden and so severe." He dashed into the cottage, and, reappearing with the burning lamp held at full arm's length, he threw it among a bank of brambles. "We must give the room a little time to clear. I take it, Watson, that you have no longer a shadow of a doubt as to how these tragedies were produced?"

"None whatever."

"But the cause remains as obscure as before. Come into the arbour here and let us discuss it together. That villainous stuff seems still to linger round my throat. I think we must admit that all the evidence points to this man, Mortimer Tregennis, having been the criminal in the first tragedy, though he was the victim in the second one. We must remember, in the first place, that there is some story of a family quarrel, followed by a reconciliation. How bitter that quarrel may have been, or how hollow the reconciliation we cannot tell. When I think of Mortimer Tregennis, with the foxy face and the small shrewd, beady eyes behind the spectacles, he is not a man whom I should judge to be of a particularly forgiving disposition. Well, in the next place, you will remember that this idea of someone moving in the garden, which took our attention for a moment from the real cause of the tragedy, emanated from him. He had a motive in misleading us. Finally, if he did not throw the substance into the fire at the moment of leaving the room, who did do so? The affair happened immediately after his departure. Had anyone else come in, the family would certainly have risen from the table. Besides, in peaceful Cornwall, visitors did not arrive after ten o'clock at night. We may take it, then, that all the evidence points to Mortimer Tregennis as the culprit."

"Then his own death was suicide!"

"Well, Watson, it is on the face of it a not impossible supposition. The man who had the guilt upon his soul of having brought such a fate upon his own family might well be driven by remorse to inflict it upon himself. There are, however, some cogent reasons against it. Fortunately, there is one man in England who knows all about it, and I have made arrangements by which we shall hear the facts this afternoon from his own lips. Ah! he is a little before his time. Perhaps you would kindly step this way, Dr. Leon Sterndale. We have been conducing a chemical experiment indoors which has left our little room hardly fit for the reception of so distinguished a visitor."

I had heard the click of the garden gate, and now the majestic figure of the great African explorer appeared upon the path. He turned in some surprise towards the rustic arbour in which we sat.

"You sent for me, Mr. Holmes. I had your note about an hour ago, and I have come, though I really do not know why I should obey your summons."

"Perhaps we can clear the point up before we separate," said Holmes. "Meanwhile, I am much obliged to you for your courteous acquiescence. You will excuse this informal reception in the open air, but my friend Watson and I have nearly furnished an additional chapter to what the papers call the Cornish Horror, and we prefer a clear atmosphere for the present. Perhaps, since the matters which we have to discuss will affect you personally in a very intimate fashion, it is as well that we should talk where there can be no eavesdropping."

The explorer took his cigar from his lips and gazed sternly at my companion.

"I am at a loss to know, sir," he said, "what you can have to speak about which affects me personally in a very intimate fashion."

"The killing of Mortimer Tregennis," said Holmes.

For a moment I wished that I were armed. Sterndale's fierce face turned to a dusky red, his eyes glared, and the knotted, passionate veins started out in his forehead, while he sprang forward with clenched hands towards my companion. Then he stopped, and with a violent effort he resumed a cold, rigid calmness, which was, perhaps, more suggestive of danger than his hot-headed outburst.

"I have lived so long among savages and beyond the law," said he, "that I have got into the way of being a law to myself. You would do well, Mr. Holmes, not to forget it, for I have no desire to do you an injury."

"Nor have I any desire to do you an injury, Dr. Sterndale. Surely the clearest proof of it is that, knowing what I know, I have sent for you and not for the police."

Sterndale sat down with a gasp, overawed for, perhaps, the first time in his adventurous life. There was a calm assurance of power in Holmes's manner which could not be withstood. Our visitor stammered for a moment, his great hands opening and shutting in his agitation.

"What do you mean?" he asked at last. "If this is bluff upon your part, Mr. Holmes, you have chosen a bad man for your experiment. Let us have no more beating about the bush. What DO you mean?"

"I will tell you," said Holmes, "and the reason why I tell you is that I hope frankness may beget frankness. What my next step may be will depend entirely upon the nature of your own defense."

"My defense?"

"Yes, sir."

"My defense against what?"

"Against the charge of killing Mortimer Tregennis."

Sterndale mopped his forehead with his handkerchief. "Upon my word, you are getting on," said he. "Do all your successes depend upon this prodigious power of bluff?"

"The bluff," said Holmes sternly, "is upon your side, Dr. Leon Sterndale, and not upon mine. As a proof I will tell you some of the facts upon which my conclusions are based. Of your return from Plymouth, allowing much of your property to go on to Africa, I will say nothing save that it first informed me that you were one of the factors which had to be taken into account in reconstructing this drama—"

"I came back—"

"I have heard your reasons and regard them as unconvincing and inadequate. We will pass that. You came down here to ask me whom I suspected. I refused to answer you. You then went to the vicarage, waited outside it for some time, and finally returned to your cottage."

"How do you know that?"

"I followed you."

"I saw no one."

"That is what you may expect to see when I follow you. You spent a restless night at your cottage, and you formed certain plans, which in the early morning you proceeded to put into execution. Leaving your door just as day was breaking, you filled your pocket with some reddish gravel that was lying heaped beside your gate."

Sterndale gave a violent start and looked at Holmes in amazement.

"You then walked swiftly for the mile which separated you from the vicarage. You were wearing, I may remark, the same pair of ribbed tennis shoes which are at the present moment upon your feet. At the vicarage you passed through the orchard and the side hedge, coming out under the window of the lodger Tregennis. It was now daylight, but the household was not yet stirring. You drew some of the gravel from your pocket, and you threw it up at the window above you."

Sterndale sprang to his feet.

"I believe that you are the devil himself!" he cried.

Holmes smiled at the compliment. "It took two, or possibly three, handfuls before the lodger came to the window. You beckoned him to come down. He dressed hurriedly and descended to his sitting-room. You entered by the window. There was an interview—a short one—during which you walked up and down the room. Then you passed out and closed the window, standing on the lawn outside smoking a cigar and watching what occurred. Finally, after the death of Tregennis, you withdrew as you had come. Now, Dr. Sterndale, how do you justify such conduct, and what were the motives for your actions? If you prevaricate or trifle with me, I give you my assurance that the matter will pass out of my hands forever."

Our visitor's face had turned ashen gray as he listened to the words of his accuser. Now he sat for some time in thought with his face sunk in his hands. Then with a sudden impulsive gesture he plucked a photograph from his breast-pocket and threw it on the rustic table before us.

"That is why I have done it," said he.

It showed the bust and face of a very beautiful woman. Holmes stooped over it.

"Brenda Tregennis," said he.

"Yes, Brenda Tregennis," repeated our visitor. "For years I have loved her. For years she has loved me. There is the secret of that Cornish seclusion which people have marvelled at. It has brought me close to the one thing on earth that was dear to me. I could not marry her, for I have a wife who has left me for years and yet whom, by the deplorable laws of England, I could not divorce. For years Brenda waited. For years I waited. And this is what we have waited for." A terrible sob shook his great frame, and he clutched his throat under his brindled beard. Then with an effort he mastered himself and spoke on:

"The vicar knew. He was in our confidence. He would tell you that she was an angel upon earth. That was why he telegraphed to me and I returned. What was my baggage or Africa to me when I learned that such a fate had come upon my darling? There you have the missing clue to my action, Mr. Holmes."

"Proceed," said my friend.

Dr. Sterndale drew from his pocket a paper packet and laid it upon the table. On the outside was written "Radix pedis diaboli" with a red poison label beneath it. He pushed it towards me. "I understand that you are a doctor, sir. Have you ever heard of this preparation?"

"Devil's-foot root! No, I have never heard of it."

"It is no reflection upon your professional knowledge," said he, "for I believe that, save for one sample in a laboratory at Buda, there is no other specimen in Europe. It has not yet found its way either into the pharmacopoeia or into the literature of toxicology. The root is shaped like a foot, half human, half goatlike; hence the fanciful name given by a botanical missionary. It is used as an ordeal poison by the medicine-men in certain districts of West Africa and is kept as a secret among them. This particular specimen I obtained under very extraordinary circumstances in the Ubangi country." He opened the paper as he spoke and disclosed a heap of reddish-brown, snuff-like powder.

"Well, sir?" asked Holmes sternly.

"I am about to tell you, Mr. Holmes, all that actually occurred, for you already know so much that it is clearly to my interest that you should know all. I have already explained the relationship in which I stood to the Tregennis family. For the sake of the sister I was friendly with the brothers. There was a family quarrel about money which estranged this man Mortimer, but it was supposed to be made up, and I afterwards met him as I did the others. He was a sly, subtle, scheming man, and several things arose which gave me a suspicion of him, but I had no cause for any positive quarrel.

"One day, only a couple of weeks ago, he came down to my cottage and I showed him some of my African curiosities. Among other things I exhibited this powder, and I told him of its strange properties, how it stimulates those brain centres which control the emotion of fear, and how either madness or death is the fate of the unhappy native who is subjected to the ordeal by the priest of his tribe. I told him also how powerless European science would be to detect it. How he took it I cannot say, for I never left the room, but there is no doubt that it was then, while I was opening cabinets and stooping to boxes, that he managed to abstract some of the devil's-foot root. I well remember how he plied me with questions as to the amount and the time that was needed for its effect, but I little dreamed that he could have a personal reason for asking.

"I thought no more of the matter until the vicar's telegram reached me at Plymouth. This villain had thought that I would be at sea before the news could reach me, and that I should be lost for years in Africa. But I returned at once. Of course, I could not listen to the details without feeling assured that my poison had been used. I came round to see you on the chance that some other explanation had suggested itself to you. But there could be none. I was convinced that Mortimer Tregennis was the murderer; that for the sake of money, and with the idea, perhaps, that if the other members of his family were all insane he would be the sole guardian of their joint property, he had used the devil's-foot powder upon them, driven two of them out of their senses, and killed his sister Brenda, the one human being whom

I have ever loved or who has ever loved me. There was his crime; what was to be his punishment?

"Should I appeal to the law? Where were my proofs? I knew that the facts were true, but could I help to make a jury of countrymen believe so fantastic a story? I might or I might not. But I could not afford to fail. My soul cried out for revenge. I have said to you once before, Mr. Holmes, that I have spent much of my life outside the law, and that I have come at last to be a law to myself. So it was even now. I determined that the fate which he had given to others should be shared by himself. Either that or I would do justice upon him with my own hand. In all England there can be no man who sets less value upon his own life than I do at the present moment.

"Now I have told you all. You have yourself supplied the rest. I did, as you say, after a restless night, set off early from my cottage. I foresaw the difficulty of arousing him, so I gathered some gravel from the pile which you have mentioned, and I used it to throw up to his window. He came down and admitted me through the window of the sitting-room. I laid his offence before him. I told him that I had come both as judge and executioner. The wretch sank into a chair, paralyzed at the sight of my revolver. I lit the lamp, put the powder above it, and stood outside the window, ready to carry out my threat to shoot him should he try to leave the room. In five minutes he died. My God! how he died! But my heart was flint, for he endured nothing which my innocent darling had not felt before him. There is my story, Mr. Holmes. Perhaps, if you loved a woman, you would have done as much yourself. At any rate, I am in your hands. You can take what steps you like. As I have already said, there is no man living who can fear death less than I do."

Holmes sat for some little time in silence.

"What were your plans?" he asked at last.

"I had intended to bury myself in central Africa. My work there is but half finished."

"Go and do the other half," said Holmes. "I, at least, am not prepared to prevent you."

Dr. Sterndale raised his giant figure, bowed gravely, and walked from the arbour. Holmes lit his pipe and handed me his pouch.

"Some fumes which are not poisonous would be a welcome change," said he. "I think you must agree, Watson, that it is not a case in which we are called upon to interfere. Our investigation has been independent, and our action shall be so also. You would not denounce the man?"

"Certainly not," I answered.

"I have never loved, Watson, but if I did and if the woman I loved had met such an end, I might act even as our lawless lion- hunter has done. Who knows? Well, Watson, I will not offend your intelligence by explaining what is obvious. The gravel upon the window-sill was, of course, the starting-point of my research. It was unlike anything in the vicarage garden. Only when my attention had been drawn to Dr. Sterndale and his cottage did I find its counterpart. The lamp shining in broad daylight and the remains of powder upon the shield were successive links in a fairly obvious chain. And now, my dear Watson, I think we may dismiss the matter from our mind and go back with a clear conscience to the study of those Chaldean roots which are surely to be traced in the Cornish branch of the great Celtic speech."

Made in United States
North Haven, CT
31 July 2022

22090560R00134